Also by Mercedes Ron

**Culpables**
*My Fault*
*Your Fault*
*Our Fault*

**Tell Me**
*Tell Me Softly*
*Tell Me in Secret*
*Tell Me with Kisses*

# Tell Me with Kisses

## MERCEDES RON

Bloom books

Published by Bloom Books, an imprint of Sourcebooks
1935 Brookdale RD, Naperville, IL 60563–2773
(630) 961-3900
sourcebooks.com

Originally self-published in 2021 by Mercedes Ron.

Cataloging-in-Publication data is on file with the Library of Congress.

The authorized representative in the EEA is Dorling Kindersley
Verlag GmbH. Arnulfstr. 124, 80636 Munich, Germany

Manufactured in the UK by Clays and distributed
by Dorling Kindersley Limited, London
001-358661-May/26
10 9 8 7 6 5 4 3 2 1

# Publisher's Note

This is a work of fiction translated from the original 2020 Spanish publication of the Dímelo series. Translation was done as closely as possible to the author's original work, characters, plot, and voice, so some liberties were taken with regard to U.S. law and the response of authorities to a school shooting.

# *Author's Note*

This book is, above all, a story of love, growth, and second chances. However, it touches on a difficult subject: a high school shooting.

My intention has always been to approach this part of the story with great care, respect, and sensitivity, knowing how deeply painful and real this kind of experience is for so many people and communities. The scene is not meant to glorify violence or dwell on it, but to reflect the emotional impact it has on the characters and how, even in moments of fear and loss, human beings reach for one another in search of comfort, connection, and hope.

If this content feels heavy for you, please take your time reading it, or step away if you need to.

Thank you for trusting this story.

Mercedes

# Content Warning

This book contains scenes of gun violence, including descriptions of a school shooting, as well as references to gun violence, sexual assault, cyberbullying, harassment, and physical assault.

# Part One

# CHAPTER ONE

## *Kami*

NO ONE HAD ANY IDEA WHERE JULIAN WAS—A WEEK HAD passed since Thiago had gone to New York and learned that the cyber-stalker, the one who was manipulating everyone and turning them against me, was Julian Murphy, a.k.a. Jules. The same guy who had invited me to watch a movie the night we went to Falls Church only to drug me, take a video of me naked, and put it on the web for everyone to see. The same guy who had caused problems between one of my best friends and me, and had uploaded photos to my Instagram after extorting my little brother to sneak into my room and steal them from me. The same person who had pretended to be gay to get close to me, who had sworn he was my friend.

I stopped pressing my pencil into the sheet of paper and ran my finger over the hole I'd just made in my drawing. I hadn't realized I was pushing down so hard.

I had been doodling randomly, and there was nothing special about the images, but if you really looked at them, they'd make your hair stand on end. Every picture I'd created lately had been creepy. But that was to be expected.

Could the year get any worse?

I doubted it. How could one person have such bad luck?

Everything happening at school had distracted me so much that I had stopped even thinking about my parents' divorce. My mother had become a mere shell of her former self, rendered unstable from all the recent events. She'd found out both her children were being bullied, and my grandmother was driving her crazy, telling her constantly she had no idea how to raise us. She was tired and worried since the money Dad sent us every month wasn't enough to maintain the lifestyle she was used to. Little by little, she was starting to have to make sacrifices.

At least now, though, she seemed a little more human and less like the stupid, superficial Barbie doll she'd always been. She didn't have time to be so self-involved since she had to manage the house, take us to school and pick us up, cook, and focus on my little brother.

She had gone with me the day before to the police station to file a report against Julian for electronic harassment, sexual assault, and unlawful dissemination of explicit images. I had been nervous about it—I wasn't sure if I would be able to handle it, to actually take him to court and try to convict a person I'd thought was my friend just a few days before. I didn't want to see him again, I couldn't, but Mom and Grandma had kept insisting, over and over. In the end, the ones who finally convinced me, though, were the Di Bianco brothers.

What was it about those two that they could penetrate my thoughts so easily? How did they always manage to make their opinions, their concept of me, matter so much that I stopped being scared? How could they persuade me in one simple conversation to do something my family had struggled and failed at?

I hadn't forgotten the moment I'd shared with Thiago in his car the day he'd found out the truth and Julian had gotten his ass beaten. I couldn't forget those green eyes looking deep into my soul to send me a message that would change everything in the depths of my subconscious mind.

He loved me.

Thiago loved me. How could he love me?

We hadn't been alone with each other since that time in his car. Taylor hadn't left my side, and Thiago was more distant than ever. The one time he spoke to me was to try and encourage me to turn Julian in. I was in Taylor's room, and I guess he heard us talking because he burst in and warned me that if I didn't do anything, I was putting hundreds of girls in danger of falling, as I had, into the trap of a manipulative, compulsive liar.

He was right. I knew that. He couldn't have been more right. So I did as he said—I went to the police station and made my statement.

What happened after that still keeps me up at night.

They went to Julian's house to arrest him, but when they got there, he was gone. His family had no idea where he was. The last time they'd seen him had been that morning, when he'd told them he was going to the library to study.

That was a week ago now.

Julian was nowhere to be found. He had vanished and

hadn't even bothered to hide the hundreds of photos he had been taking of everybody at school. They were right there in his room, along with videos, especially of the basketball team and the cheerleading squad. But I was clearly the one he'd really fixated on.

He had taken hundreds of photos and videos of me without my knowledge and had stolen private pictures of mine, including images of me as a little girl. Had he been following me, spying on me, for that long?

Julian was a psychopath. A psychopath obsessed with me.

I had tried to get close to Kate again—she was his sister; she had to know something—but even though she used to be my best friend, she refused to talk to me now. Ellie told me Kate had quit the cheerleading squad, and barely anyone had seen her since Julian's secrets came out.

I'd had my eye on her in the days leading up to that weekend, and I could tell something wasn't right. I figured it hadn't been easy for her to find out that her stepbrother was a fucking stalker. It's not like Julian and Kate got along that well. In fact, they could hardly stand one another, but he was still her brother.

On the day Julian was beaten up by the mob of angry students, Taylor had managed to slip away into the crowd at the last second, avoiding the punishment the others got. They were suspended, including Danny. As far as I was concerned, Taylor should have been suspended, too. Every action had a consequence.

But he'd gotten away with it.

I closed my drawing pad and tucked it into my desk

drawer. As always, I looked out the window to the next house over, where the cause of my sweetest dreams and my worst nightmares laid his head.

Thiago had been avoiding me ever since that day in his car when he confessed that he loved me. Every day since then, every cell in my body had been longing to be by his side once more. Have you ever felt the pain that comes from physically needing someone? The way your body begs for their warmth alone to restore its vitality? That's how I felt.

Whenever I went to see Taylor and we crossed through the living room to go upstairs, Thiago was always there, lying on the couch watching TV or sleeping with his face on his forearm. Sometimes, I'd peek into his room from the landing, and there he'd be, reading a book or sitting in front of his computer, or—God forbid—doing push-ups shirtless with his music on full blast.

That killed me.

It killed me every time we crossed paths and I couldn't cover him in kisses.

We looked but didn't touch. I'm not going to lie. Our eyes hungered for each other. We needed a dose of each other just to get through the day. And that scared me.

Taylor was caring, attentive to my every need, and he was terrified that Julian might show up out of the blue and try to hurt me. His and Thiago's relationship was colder than ever. They barely spoke, and Taylor seemed set on avoiding Thiago's company—especially if *I* was around.

That made things hard because I still thought about Thiago all the time. I could hardly control my anxiety; I needed to know how he was doing. I missed him, and however hard I wished I could stop feeling that, it was impossible.

At least we still had the window.

There had been a time when he used to close the curtains to shut me out. Not anymore. Now they were always open, and I could see him whenever I wanted. I left mine open, too. They were big floor-to-ceiling windows that let in tons of light. Would you believe I had actually moved my bed? So when I lay there, trying to sleep, I could look out and see Thiago doing the same.

I was losing it; I knew that. But I needed him. It was as simple as that.

———

Monday was gray and windy. I got up at seven thirty, looked outside, and a chill ran through me. All I wanted was to crawl back into bed. It's hard to leave the warmth of your blankets and the shelter of your room when all that's awaiting you is a long day of classes and presentations—and nothing to look forward to at three o'clock but gray skies and rain.

But that was how it was. And I needed to try to get things back to normal.

My "friends"—I use quotation marks because I wasn't sure how true their friendship was—had started talking to me again. I had the feeling, deep down, that they were only doing it because I'd become the talk of the town, thanks to Julian, and they, like everyone else, wanted to get more details out of me.

The real story had gotten buried under so many layers

of lies that there were even people saying they'd seen Julian hiding out in the woods behind my house or walking around town after midnight with a rifle in hand. Some idiot spread the rumor that Julian wore a disguise and still came to school incognito.

Tall tales, that's all they were.

But people were nervous, anxious, and I was worried, too: that he might reveal hidden secrets about the other students, ruin people's lives, their reputations...

Julian was Carsville High's worst nightmare, and yet, weirdly, even though everyone was scared of him, they seemed to admire him, too. I think they were in awe that somehow one single student had managed to cause such an uproar, hacking into people's phones and computers. My best friend, Ellie, was one of his victims.

She'd asked me to come over to her place that morning and ride with her to school so she could tell me what had really happened with her and Julian—how he had managed to get her to avoid me *and* convinced her to hook up with Danny, my asshole ex-boyfriend. She was scared, just like the rest of us who had been caught in Julian's web. I knew she wouldn't want to go into details, but I wasn't going to let her off the hook.

I texted Taylor to let him know he didn't need to pick me up, put on my warmest coat, my red hat, and my gloves, and left early, while my mother and brother were still asleep. My grandmother had gone home a few days ago, but with the promise that she'd be checking in on us to make sure no one messed with her family again.

Outside, it was as cold as the arctic. It had snowed the night before, and there were huge mounds piled up around all the houses and trees where snowplows had been clearing the streets since early that morning. The sidewalks were still glistening white, which meant I had to walk in the road. It was before sunrise, but I didn't care. I needed a few minutes to myself. Sometimes, being alone is just what your mind needs, and since everything with Julian had gone down, nobody would leave me alone. People stared at me as if I were a time bomb about to explode, and all I wanted was for things to go back to the way they'd been before.

I looked around at the winter wonderland, admiring the precious place where I'd grown up. A lot of people said Carsville was a boring small town, but I had always liked being surrounded by nature. I loved Christmas with snowmen in the woods and summer afternoons swimming in the lake. Once we got older, we'd go there to party without the watchful eyes of adults. I loved nights camped out in the yard, looking at the stars, away from the city lights that made them difficult to see.

Carsville: a place where nothing happened, would soon be on everyone's radar.

I got to Ellie's house with enough time to talk before we had to go to school. When I rang the doorbell, I figured she'd be having breakfast. Her dad opened the door. He was a tall guy with dark, curly hair. Mr. Webber's size sure made him intimidating, but I knew deep down he was nothing but a puppy dog.

"Hey, Kami! How have you been?" he asked as he

motioned for me to come inside. "C'mon in, quick, it's chilly out this morning! Did you walk all the way here?"

"Good morning, Mr. Webber. Yeah, I was in the mood for a walk. Is Ellie around?" I asked with a smile.

"Yeah, she's having breakfast," he said, hanging my coat, hat, gloves, and scarf on the coat tree in the vestibule. The heat inside was stifling, and I wanted to strip off more layers. I was already sweating as I followed Mr. Webber into the kitchen.

Ellie's house wasn't big. There was just room enough for her parents, two cats, and her. She used to always tell me how she envied my big bedroom, the huge TV in my living room, and our impressive staircase. She always wanted to come over to my house, and I always wanted to go somewhere else, to get away from the imposing decor. I usually found an excuse to end up at her place, and Mrs. Webber made one hell of an apple pie. Her house might have been small, but it was homey and always smelled of coffee and fresh-baked bread. I guess the grass is always greener on the other side.

As I entered the cozy kitchen, with its round table in the corner and light wood cabinets with little stencils of lemons, Ellie looked up from her cereal bowl with surprise, asking, "Why are you here so early?"

Her mother looked up from her newspaper and smiled. "Hello, dear! Long time no see! Can I get you some coffee? Tea? Hot chocolate? Just give me a few minutes..." She stood, laid her newspaper on the table, and walked over to the stove, ready to make whatever I asked. That was just like Mrs. Webber.

"I'd love a coffee," I told her, smiling, because I knew if I didn't accept something, she'd have gone on listing options for the rest of the day. I sat down next to Ellie and asked her, "What do you think about walking to school?"

I hoped she'd say yes, but she hesitated: "Don't you think it's a bad idea, considering that..." She trailed off.

Ellie's parents had no idea what had been going on. Since she hadn't been directly involved, the principal hadn't gotten in touch with them the way he had with my parents and Taylor and Thiago's mom. Ellie had decided not to inform them because she didn't want them worrying about a crazy kid on the loose, blackmailing half the student body.

"It's just twenty minutes," I told her, hoping she'd notice how much I needed her company.

She nodded, but I could tell she was nervous. And that made sense. We were all scared and angry at Julian for what he'd done.

As we finished breakfast with Ellie's parents, I told myself that Julian was harmless. I hated him for what he'd done, for the lies and manipulation, but I was convinced it ended there. His cruelty, his conniving, the way he'd hurt people, were all the actions of a coward, carried out from a distance, hiding his real identity.

Julian wasn't the type to confront us on the street and try to harm us.

At least, that's what I told myself.

When breakfast was over, we bundled up and headed outside. Ellie's father usually drove her in, and he didn't like the idea of us being out in the cold, but we managed to convince him.

Once we were finally alone, walking side by side in the bike lane, I could sense that my worries about Ellie weren't wrong. Something was going on with her. And that something had to do with me.

"Listen, Ellie..." I said after a brief uncomfortable silence, only interrupted by the chirping of birds and one or two passing cars. "Do you have some kind of problem with me?" I said, cutting to the point. I didn't want to feel awkward around my best friend, especially not now that I needed her more than ever...

She didn't speak for a few seconds, then she told me, "I'm really sorry for what happened with Julian, Kami." She was looking at the ground, as though she didn't have the courage to meet my gaze.

"What do you mean, exactly?"

"You know he forced me to do things I'd never have done otherwise..."

Like hooking up with Danny at the Halloween party. How could I forget! I still had nightmares about the two of them together, not because I was jealous, but because my best friend, someone I loved and respected, had gone after the maniac who'd made my life impossible for two years. It made me angry, but it made me sad, too.

Danny didn't deserve someone like Ellie.

And Ellie... She deserved the best. A good guy, someone fun, someone who could make her laugh, get under her skin, push her to do things she'd never do on her own.

She deserved the best guy in the world, which I told her straight up. Ellie looked off at the trees and said, "What if the perfect guy's out of my reach?" Then she turned back to face me.

"Ellie, no decent guy with a brain would turn you down," I responded. She was a total catch: smart, pretty, fun, sweet. She looked at me skeptically, hinting that she had her eye on someone. I shouted, "Oh my God, who is it? Do I know him? Is it someone from our class?"

I went through all the guys at school in my head, and no one jumped out as someone even remotely in her league, but hey—if there was someone she liked, I wasn't going to be the one to burst her bubble.

"We've got some classes with him..." she responded, even more nervous than before. Dammit! Who was it?

"Ellie, spit it out!" I said when we were almost to school.

I could tell she was hesitant, but at last, she took a breath and said, "Sorry, Kami, it's just... I don't want you to hate me. It's not like I planned this or anything. Feelings, you know, they just appear out of nowhere, and I didn't see this coming..."

Just as she was about to say more, a car honked, and we both nearly jumped out of our skin. "Jesus!" I shouted, and noticed it was Thiago and Taylor pulling into school. We watched them turn as we kept walking. The brothers parked at the edge of the lot, far from the school building but close to us.

I could feel the nerves in the pit of my stomach as Thiago

got out of the driver's side, slamming the door and turning toward me. Taylor did the same from the passenger side.

"What have you done now?" Ellie asked.

I froze: They were headed straight for me, with angry expressions on their handsome faces.

"You want to tell me what the fuck you're doing walking to school by yourself?" Believe it or not, it wasn't my boyfriend, Taylor, who asked. It was his brother, Thiago.

I was stunned. Thiago was like a bulldozer; he couldn't control his temper. I looked at Taylor, and he was pissed, too, but part of that was his anger at being upstaged by his brother.

Thiago was going too far. I think sometimes he forgot that I was going out with his brother, not him.

"What am I supposed to do?" I shouted. "I wanted to take a walk with my best friend!"

"Your best friend can do whatever she wants. You're a different story!" he shouted, standing just inches away from me. God, he was so tall, so strong, so fucking irresistible.

I looked to Taylor for help. "Can you get your brother to stop yelling at me?" The last thing I needed was somebody else making a spectacle of me at school. Thankfully we were at least far enough from the doors that no one could gawk at us except the last few people pulling into the parking lot.

"Sorry, Kami, but not this time. I hate to say it, but he's right. It's pretty stupid to walk around alone when you know an absolute psycho has you in his sights!" Taylor said.

I couldn't believe he was talking to me this way. Before

I could answer, Ellie hissed, "You can't talk to her like that." She was clearly pissed at how they were treating me.

I don't think Taylor had realized she was there. Now he turned to her and said, "Beat it. I want to talk to my girlfriend one on one." The message was clearly intended for Thiago, too.

I was surprised at how easily I could read Thiago's mind as he looked back and forth between us. I saw pain, anger, rage, helplessness—and I saw him wanting to claim me as his. But he couldn't. I wanted to confront him, I wanted to tell him off, but my heart was split in two. As always, it was impossible to be logical when he was around.

"Kami," Ellie said, "feel free to leave these two dumbasses and come in with me. You don't have to explain anything to them. You felt like walking to school. It's none of their business."

Taylor turned to her. "What part of the phrase *Beat it* did you not understand?"

He was seething, and she was hurt, but she was trying hard to cover it up. My mind quickly put the pieces together.

Ellie liked Taylor.

That was what she hadn't wanted to tell me…and that was how Julian had blackmailed her.

"What part of *It's none of your business* don't you understand?" she fired back.

Before he could say something nasty to her again, I cut him off: "Taylor, stop. It was my decision to walk to school, and I'm not going to live my life in fear of some high school freak. If Julian had actually wanted to hurt me, he had a thousand chances to do it, and he didn't! You guys see him as some kind of danger, but for me, he's just a pathetic loser who had to lie to me and lie to himself to make friends. He's a creep, a liar. He's a pathetic asshole, and he's going to spend the rest of his life alone. And now, if you don't mind, I'd like to get to class with my best friend."

Thiago looked like he wanted to drag me away and chew me out. But I didn't care now. I grabbed Ellie's hand and started walking off. No sooner had I taken two steps than Taylor stopped me, clutching my arm. "We need to talk," he demanded, pursing his lips.

Thiago tried to jump in again, but I didn't want the situation to get any worse. Dealing with two angry brothers was too much, especially when they were vying for my attention. To calm things down, I said, "Taylor, we'll talk in biology class." My tone was curt, and I saw on his face that he understood he'd gone too far.

He let me go, but tension still lingered in the air as I walked away.

———

My first class was hell—math, of course—and to make things worse, I still hadn't been able to talk to Ellie about what I was certain I'd just figured out. Mr. Gomez was a hothead, and he hated students talking in class. I remember one time he caught two people passing notes, and he made them take an extra quiz each week for a whole month. That added up to half their grade! It sounds crazy, but he didn't bat an eye about it.

Plus, Ellie didn't seem to want to talk to me. She just looked straight ahead and noted down everything the teacher said without giving me the time of day. We had barely spoken since our confrontation with the Di Bianco brothers. I had tried my hardest to get her to open up, but all she had to say was, "Kami, we're going to be late to class! This is no time to get into it!"

It mattered to me, though. I had been so wrapped up in my parents' divorce, the harassment I'd suffered, my friendship with Julian, going out with Taylor, hooking up with Thiago, and everything else, that I'd barely paid attention to her. And I knew that was wrong.

I promised myself I would go back to being the person I'd been before, at least when it came to my friendships. I couldn't just throw aside the people I had history with. And realizing that made me think of Kate.

Did Kate know what her brother had been up to? Had she known he was manipulating all of us? Had she helped him dig up dirty secrets on half the people at our school?

I wanted to know, and I wasn't the only one. Lots of people were convinced the two of them had been in cahoots, and more than a few people had turned their back on her. They sneered and scowled at her, and it almost seemed as if they were taking everything out on her since Julian had disappeared. Ellie had even joked about how the illegitimate queen had fallen, and now I could retake my throne. I hated her saying that, it sounded so superficial, but I knew it was just her way of finding humor in everything that we'd gone through.

I didn't want to be on any throne, though, especially not among the cheerleaders. I didn't want attention. I didn't want anything to do with that school, actually. I just wanted to finish the year and go to college and never look back. These kinds of things didn't happen at college—people were more mature, and parents weren't around all the time scheming to take away your freedom. That was exactly what I needed.

To start from zero.

Taylor popped into my head. He wanted to go to Harvard; I wanted to go to Yale. That would be a problem, but I was relieved to think I wouldn't be the only one who would have to deal with it. Everyone knew that if you started a relationship your senior year of high school, you had to accept that it might end. Most couples couldn't handle the distance, especially not at college, with all that newfound freedom that often went to people's heads, driving them to cheat or break up with someone…

I tried to tell myself that what I had with Taylor wouldn't end that way. But with my heart still longing for Thiago, I'd started to believe that I didn't deserve either of them. And yet I was too weak to let them go.

Did that make me the worst person in the world?

I think the answer's pretty damn clear.

# CHAPTER TWO

## *Taylor*

I WAITED OUTSIDE HER MATH CLASS TO TALK TO HER. I WAS still angry, but she'd gotten to school safely, so I had started to let it go. There was something else that mattered more, and that was making sure nothing happened to her in the future.

I didn't care what she said or thought about Julian. I knew the truth: He was dangerous, and something inside me told me that his story was far from finished.

I leaned against the wall across from her classroom and saw the two of them come out together. They looked tense. Ellie was starting to get on my nerves. Why couldn't she just mind her own business? I got it—they were friends and she was just defending Kami. But she didn't have to be so hostile toward me.

Ellie's smile turned to a defiant scowl as soon as she saw me. I just looked at her blankly and turned to Kami. One look at her and I felt like I could lose my mind in every sense imaginable. Kami stopped and glanced back and forth between us. Since she looked like she was struggling to decide, I stepped forward and said, "Can we talk?"

Kami hesitated, then nodded and told Ellie, "See you in history."

Ellie nodded, giving me another nasty look, and walked toward her locker.

I wrapped an arm around Kami's waist and pulled her toward me, resting my back against the wall as I buried my head in her neck and she did the same, melting into me as I inhaled her sweet fragrance.

I had been so scared when she'd told me not to pick her up this morning. My imagination had gotten the better of me. I'd pictured dozens of scary situations I still couldn't manage to shake.

"Do me a favor, please," I told her. "Don't do that again."

"I didn't do anything, Taylor," she said, and I could tell by how sharply she reacted that she was still angry at my brother and me for what we'd said.

"Is it really too much to ask that you not cross the entire town alone?" I asked. What I wanted was to grab her by the shoulders and shake some sense into her. "Julian is out there somewhere, and the police aren't taking it seriously. They think he's just some emotional teenager, but I know he's dangerous. And he's going to come back. This isn't over, Kamila." I thought maybe calling her by her full name would help her see how serious I was. I couldn't understand why it was so hard for her to realize she was truly in danger. The extent of that danger, I didn't know, but I didn't want to find out the hard way. I couldn't let anything bad happen to her.

Kami stepped away from me and crossed her arms. "I wasn't alone, Ellie was with me."

"Ellie doesn't count, Kami. If Julian shows up, what could she do about it?"

"Ellie's amazing, Taylor! How can you say that about her?" Her sudden outburst caught me off guard, and I tried to explain myself, but she cut me off: "And by the way, I don't like how you're treating her. It wouldn't kill you to be nice once in a while. She is my best friend, you know. That should be worth something."

"I care about you," I said, trying to be as stern and serious as she was.

"I'm fine," she said, stepping back. "You have nothing to worry about. What happened with Julian is over, and the only thing I want is to forget it, but it's hard when you and your brother can't stop reminding me of it every second of the day."

I took a deep breath and tried to calm down. If it was up to me, there would be a whole army following her around to make sure she was OK. But that was impossible, and so it was up to my brother and me. Obviously, I wasn't thrilled about including Thiago because the farther he was from Kami, the better. But I needed his help. In the end, there was no one I trusted more to keep her safe.

"We're worried about you," I said, hearing the urgency in my own voice.

Kami ran her hand down my cheek in a soft caress and delicately kissed me on the lips.

"I know," she said, and her breath tickled my skin. "And I appreciate it. I really do, and I promise I'll be careful, but please, relax a little."

When she put it like that, I couldn't say no, and I agreed, pulling her in for a real kiss. Her body curved into mine, and I pressed my tongue into her mouth to taste her slowly. I got hard almost instantly and remembered we'd still only done it once. Every pore in my body was screaming to do it again, soon, and she knew it...but she was avoiding it. My hands moved down to her ass, pressing my erection into her, but she wriggled away.

"Tay, no, not here," she said, removing my hands and smiling at me, blushing.

God, she was gorgeous.

I stroked her blond hair, wishing we could be anywhere else, just the two of us alone, with no one bothering us, somewhere we could have sex and then curl up to sleep together. Somewhere I could wake up and make her breakfast the next morning.

Sometimes it sucks being seventeen.

"We're going to be late," she warned me, kissing me on the cheek. "And today we find out which day we have our human sexuality presentation."

I couldn't help but raise my eyebrows flirtatiously. "I'm sorry, are you telling me I need to put time aside to work on my sexuality with you?"

She laughed and rolled her eyes. "We've been working

on this assignment for a month and you're still coming up with new material. Incredible. You're a child."

"A horny child who can't stop thinking about giving it to you again," I said, unable to stop myself.

"Taylor!" Kami giggled adorably, looking back and forth to see if anyone in the hallway had heard us.

"What?" I asked. "Are you offended by my vulgar comments?"

"I'm just surprised by how horny you are."

"Says the girl who was begging for it the other day…"

She put her hand over my mouth, telling me to shut up before I could say any more. I stuck my tongue out and licked her palm, and she pulled her hand back, wiping it on her shirt, and shouted, "Gross!"

"Come on," I said, looking at my watch, "we're late."

Noting the time, Kami opened her eyes in horror, then took my hand as we ran to biology class.

The students were all already inside and seated, and when we opened the door, we were surprised to find not Ms. Davies's gentle smile—but my older brother's cold stare, waving us in. Kami froze as they stared at each other. It was impossible to say what the meaning of that look was.

"You're ten minutes late," Thiago said, shaking his head.

"Sorry," Kami replied, pulling me over to our table. As soon as we'd sat down, I noticed Thiago was actually furious, and the rest of the class had picked up on that, too. They seemed to be waiting for a fight to break out.

"And just why are you late?" Thiago asked.

"I don't think they were playing Parcheesi, Coach," Victor Di Viani said, and everyone laughed.

Kami nudged me with her elbow and pointed at her lips. Shit! I wiped my mouth with the back of my sleeve, and a big streak of Kami's lipstick rubbed off on it. I tried to avoid my brother's stare as I shot a nasty glance at Victor. I might just kick his ass later.

"That's detention for both of you," Thiago said indifferently. "I'll see you after class."

"Come on!" I couldn't believe it.

"That will give you time to make up what you missed during the first ten minutes of class."

"Taylor's already got his makeup on," Di Viani said.

I clenched my fists. I was going to kill that jerk.

"Di Viani, that's detention for you, too," my brother said, taking some papers out of his bag. That, at least, took the edge off my anger. Victor sat there, dumbfounded. I wondered what was up with my brother. There were times when it seemed like he couldn't care less about anyone around him.

That wasn't the case with Kami, though. She hadn't taken her eyes off him since he mentioned detention.

"I work this afternoon," she said.

Thiago looked up at her. For a few seconds, he said nothing, then he responded, "Do I look like someone who wants to hear your life story?" A hush fell over the class, silent as a funeral.

"I can't miss work," Kami said, sitting up tense in her chair, her face filled with dread.

"Thiago, it won't happen again," I cut in. This whole thing was starting to piss me off. I mean, he was my fucking brother. Couldn't he just chill out for once?

"Whether it happens again depends on whether you're capable of learning that actions have consequences, and we'll only find that out after you've served your detention."

"You're not even our teacher," Kami objected. "If Ms. Davies were here, she wouldn't even care." She was starting to raise her voice.

"Yeah, well, here's some news for you: Life is unfair, and I'm your teacher today," Thiago retorted, clearly unfazed. "And I'd like to start class now. I hear Ms. Davies assigned you guys a project. Today I'll tell you the order you're to present in…"

"Look, Thiago, I'm not going to detention. Sorry, but there's no way I'm going to lose my job just because I was ten minutes late to class," Kami announced, interrupting him again.

She crossed her arms, and my brother looked up from the list in his hands. "Kamila, get out of my classroom," he ordered her.

"It's not your classroom," she fired back.

I squeezed her thigh under the table, trying to calm her down. I knew Thiago, and talking to him like that in front of all the other students was a truly bad idea.

"Out," he repeated, pointing at the door.

Kami stood up so fast her chair made a screeching sound. She grabbed her books and her bag and walked out, slamming the door. Thiago shut his eyes for a second and took a deep breath. Then he looked straight at me. I was glaring at him, but he didn't seem to care. He stood up and started reading off the list of projects.

I was livid. I knew he wasn't really punishing us for being tardy. He was still pissed about Kami walking to school while Julian was still out there. And Thiago knew that if Kami spent the afternoon with him, Julian couldn't get to her.

He was punishing her, but he was also protecting her.

A part of me wished I had the power to do the same.

# CHAPTER THREE

## Kami

I WALKED OUT WITHOUT LOOKING BACK. I KNOW IT WAS rude, I know I should have controlled myself, but I couldn't stand him acting that way with me. It didn't make sense! Or maybe it did, because ever since we'd confessed our feelings, we couldn't seem to stop being pissed at each other, except when we were stealing glances through our bedroom windows. Were we mad because we couldn't act on our feelings? Were we just taking it out on the one person who mattered most? And did those stolen glances really mean anything if we were constantly acting like we hated each other?

I walked down the hall toward the library, thinking I'd study a bit, when behind me, I heard a door creak open. I stopped and turned. It was Thiago.

I studied him carefully as he came over. He was dressed in jeans, a shirt and tie, and a navy-blue sweater vest. He looked like the classic sexy professor, and he was driving me wild, but of course I had to try my best to pretend he wasn't affecting me.

"What?" I asked. "Are you here to say sorry?"

He grinned. Did he think this was funny? "I'll move your detention to your free period. Every day for the rest of the month. That way, you won't have to miss work," he said.

"What made you change your mind?" I asked with crossed arms.

"I'll be in my office in the gym, not in the teacher's lounge, FYI," he said, without answering my question, looking down at me like I was a child.

"So?"

"Wait for me there, for your detention."

He turned around and walked away, and I called after him, unable to help myself: "You know, you're taking this way too far."

He stopped and said blithely, "See you during your free period, Kamila." Then he disappeared into the classroom, and I stormed off to the library, practically steaming.

Every free period for a month!

I headed into the library and saw that one of two plush chairs was unoccupied. All the students fought over these spots during exam season since the other tables just had hard wooden seats. There was no better place to flop down, stay warm, and study. But since classes were in session, there were only a few people in there: seniors who had their free period and were studying for finals, which would start in December and could count for as much as 70 percent of our grades. Everyone was cramming like mad, including Kate, apparently. I saw her just past the last shelf by the window, sitting in one of the plush chairs. In her lap was her history book, and she looked mesmerized. And haggard. And incredibly sad. When I got close, she glanced up, surprised.

"You mind if I sit down?" I asked, pointing at the empty chair next to her.

She looked over and started gathering her things. "Sure, I was just about to go."

As she started to stand, I said, "No, please, Kate, don't go. I'm just here looking for a little peace and quiet. I mean, I'm also here because I got kicked out of class."

I was hoping to find a way to connect with her. "What?" she asked. "They kicked you out of class? You?"

Her comment showed how little we'd talked recently. Whatever reputation I had for staying out of trouble was gone at this point. I'd almost gotten kicked out of school over fights and other problems I hadn't even started.

"Yeah, me," I said, sitting down, seeing that at least for now she'd given up on her idea of leaving.

"Who was your teacher?"

"Thiago Di Bianco," I responded sarcastically.

"He's a teacher now?"

"Sub. I was ten minutes late to class and he told me I had to give up my free period for the rest of the month."

"I was twenty minutes late to PE the other day and he didn't say a word," she said.

Now that pissed me off. "He's a jerk," I said, rubbing my hands together by the heater to warm them. For a few seconds, we sat there in an awkward silence until I gathered the courage to say, "Kate, are you OK?"

She blinked several times and replied in a thin voice, "Yeah, I'm great. Why do you ask?"

I hesitated, then answered, "What happened with your brother must have been hard for you."

"Stepbrother," she corrected me.

I could have corrected her in turn—he was her half brother, not her stepbrother. They had the same dad. But who was I to criticize her for wanting to create some separation between herself and the most manipulative person I'd ever met?

"I'm fine," she went on. "It's just that people want to blame me for what happened, and it's not fair."

"It isn't," I agreed. "But do you have any idea why he did it? Or where he might have gone?"

She froze for a second, then leaped up. "You honestly think I know where he is? Are you fucking for real? Did you come here to try to get information out of me? Because I don't know, OK? I don't know!" She was shouting, and everyone nearby turned in surprise.

"Hey! I'm sorry, Kate, OK?" I held up my hands, frightened by how drastic her reaction had been. Her eyes bulged from their sockets, and I even began to wonder if she might be high.

"Don't say you're sorry, just leave me alone!" she shrieked, turning away and stomping out of the library.

I hid my head in the pages of my biology textbook and tried to pretend nothing had happened. Everyone in the library was staring at me, and by the time my free period came, everyone seemed to have heard about my run-in with

Kate. Outside, a couple of girls stopped me to ask about it, and even Ellie ran over wanting to gossip.

"Ellie," I told her, "I didn't do anything, I swear. She got hysterical. I mean, I've never seen her like that before, and Kate's always been a drama queen," I said as we walked toward the gym. Ellie must have zoned out as I was talking, because once we were inside, she asked, "What are we doing here?"

"Thiago gave me detention," I said, "and I'm supposed to serve it during my study period. And shit! I'm late again."

As I pushed the door open, Ellie asked, "Thiago?" She was just as surprised as Kate had been.

"I'll tell you later. Besides, you've still got secrets to tell me!"

She pretended not to hear this last part, and as I started in, I ran smack into a wall of muscle. "Shit!" I yelled, standing back and smelling his fragrance all over me.

"You're late again?"

I stepped back to try and clear my head and studied him. He'd taken off his vest and loosened his tie, and his sleeves were rolled up. "I think you're taking this sub position a little too seriously," I commented.

"I don't have class until after lunch. Follow me," he ordered. The gym was empty, and I realized we were going to be alone. With the snowy weather, a dim light filtered through the windows.

He kept the office much neater than Coach Klebb had. That didn't surprise me. Thiago was uptight about those things; he always wanted everything perfectly in order, or *perfectly in disorder* as he liked to say when talking about his special way of arranging his stuff. There was a desk, the whiteboard where he mapped out the team's plays, and in one corner a bunch of fitness equipment and a pile of deflated balls. Thiago sat down, grabbed a pencil, and started writing something on a sheet of paper. I stood there, unsure of what to do.

"I want you to blow up those balls and repair the ones that have holes in them. There's some special tape over there," he said.

"Are you serious?" I asked. "You want me to blow up all those balls?"

"Yep," he responded curtly, then looked at me with his green eyes. "What did you think, you were just going to sit here staring off into space?"

"Yeah," I said, gritting my teeth. "That's what we normally do when we have detention."

"Well, not with me." He set his pencil down and turned all his attention to me. "This will help you learn to listen to what you're instructed to do instead of showing me up in front of the other students."

"I said what I said because you were being unfair."

He half grinned. "There's a lot of unfairness in the world, Kamila. I'm not sure this counts, though."

"All I did was show up ten minutes late," I objected loudly.

"No. What you did is put yourself in danger unnecessarily," he said, now more somber.

So this was about the morning! "Seriously?! You're

actually punishing me for walking to school?" I was shouting now. I couldn't believe this. At least Taylor had finally realized he was overreacting. Thiago just kept on going with his same hard-ass attitude and nodded.

"Exactly," he said. "Maybe this way, you won't do it again."

"Is that a threat?"

"Mmmm...yeah, I think it is."

"Stop being such a dick, Thiago." I wanted to pick up one of those balls and throw it at his head.

"How about you stop driving me insane?"

That caught me off guard. I paused for a second before saying, "I drive you insane, huh?"

Our eyes met, and I smiled smugly as he gulped. "Get to work on those balls," he said.

Walking over to his desk, heart racing, I pressed him, "Answer me first. Because you've barely said more than two words to me in the last few weeks."

"Wasn't what we said the last time we were alone enough for you?"

The last time we were together he'd said *I love you.* We'd both said *I love you.*

Fuuuuuck.

"What was the point of it, though, if we're just going to treat each other like this?" I dared to ask, feeling the sharp pain of longing but unable to act on it.

"Like what?" he asked, standing up and walking around the table. Now we were close enough to touch.

"You know what I mean..."

"Alone in the same room during free period every day for the next month?"

"What?" I asked.

"You heard me."

I blinked with surprise and responded, "You're not telling me that…"

"Yeah, I am. I couldn't resist the temptation to have you all to myself for at least half an hour…" He shrugged, and my heart froze for a moment.

"You punished me because you wanted to spend time with me?"

"No," he replied, standing very still, his eyes roving over every inch of my body. "I did it because I'm fucking furious with you, and I had to do something to calm myself down. Punishing you felt like a gratifying way to do it. Getting to spend a free period with you was the cherry on top."

"So I'm the cherry?" I couldn't help but ask.

"And a very sweet one at that," he said, and by the way he shifted his weight, I could tell he was dying to touch me, hold me, kiss me…

I stepped forward, but he didn't move. I took another step, averting his gaze, and rested my forehead on his chest. I took a deep breath, trying to calm my impulses, and just as I was preparing to move away, he placed his hand on the back of my head. Then he ran his fingers through my hair and kissed me on the top of my head as he inhaled the scent of my shampoo.

"You've got a choice to make," he whispered, so softly I could hardly hear him.

Something clicked in my head. Was he asking me what I thought he was asking me? Thiago must have sensed what I was thinking, because he let me go suddenly, as if my skin were on fire.

"I'm sorry, forget what I just said." He returned to his desk.

"We can't just—" I replied in shock.

"I know," he interrupted me icily.

Looking at the ground, I imagined Taylor. Taylor, my ideal guy, who adored me and took care of me.

"I can't hurt him," I said, hoping Thiago would agree, but instead he gave me a cold stare.

"You already are, Kamila. You think he doesn't realize what's going on? And he doesn't even know the half of it."

"It's not like you and I could ever make it work," I said, waving my hands around. "They offered you a permanent position. You know I'd never endanger that for you."

"You'll be going to college in a few months. After that, it won't be a problem."

"Yeah, except for the fact that I'll be hundreds of miles away," I replied, attempting to convince myself that I was right and there was no future for us. It was impossible.

"What do you want, then, Kamila?" he asked, tossing his pencil on the table, where it bounced and rolled toward my feet. "I'm tired of this, I'm tired of pining for you day and night, watching you sleep with another guy. And not just any guy, my goddamn brother, whom I happen to adore."

Those words pierced my heart. "What's the solution, then?" I asked.

"There isn't one," he replied calmly. "And you know why?"

I waited, and finally he replied: "Because you don't even know what you want. Do you think I don't watch you two, that I don't see how you look at him? How he makes you laugh. Hell, I can hear you across the hall when I'm in my room. Deep down, I know you deserve that, I know he can offer you so much more than I ever could."

"Don't say that, Thiago." I moved closer to try and touch him, but he raised a hand, keeping me at bay.

"There's something broken inside me," he admitted, his expression completely sincere. "And there always will be. That's just who I am. Call it fate, but I'm just someone who can't run from my past."

"We all have our demons," I told him.

"It's not just my demons, though. I have my whole family's demons. And my guardian angel isn't strong enough to keep them away."

My eyes filled with tears when I realized he was talking about Lucy. She would always be the shadow he could never outrun. A shadow cast over all of us: me, Taylor, their mother—but Thiago most of all. He would never get over it. And I wished with all my heart that her shadow wouldn't destroy us, but it was always there, looming.

I walked to the other side of the room, and he watched me in silence. I waited a moment and finally spoke: "Do I really have to blow up these balls?"

Without looking at me, Thiago said, "Yep."

# CHAPTER FOUR

## Thiago

I COULDN'T RESIST.

I couldn't resist the chance to be alone with her, even if it was just for half an hour. And when I saw the chance, I took it without thinking twice. I missed her—her laughter, her silliness, everything about her. Maybe I couldn't touch her or kiss her, but I could still have her near me. And I needed that.

I thought I'd lose my mind when Taylor told me she'd walked to school. I wanted to shake some sense into her and ask her how she could be so stupid, so irresponsible, so reckless. Didn't she realize Julian was crazy? He was on the loose and obsessed with her.

To say the cops were doing a shitty job was an understatement. They weren't doing their job at all. They'd minimized it, calling it kid stuff. C'mon! Was it kid stuff to drug a girl and record her, and post the images online? Was it kid stuff to blackmail high school students to get information out of them?

The whole thing gave me a bad feeling, and I knew deep down that Julian would pop back up sooner or later. What scared me was that he might come for Kam. I loved her, and she refused to admit how dangerous things could get if Julian found her on one of her goddamned walks through the woods.

And now I had her sitting in the corner of my office, inflating balls for gym class and kicking them away noisily when she was done. She was trying to provoke me, but I wasn't going to play that game. She thought she was angry?

Well, I was even angrier.

The things we said to each other, everything we'd talked about just two weeks ago—had I lost my mind? Hadn't I promised myself I'd consider her off-limits? Then why was I so dead set on getting close to her?

Nothing could happen between us. When would I get that through my head?

I glanced over at her. She was staring out the window. I guess she'd decided she was tired of following my orders. Her light-blond hair hung loosely at her shoulders. She kept toying with it distractedly, pulling it up and letting it fall. That was something she did when she was bored or stressed, I'd noticed.

More than once, I'd stood at my window watching her, and it wasn't lost on me that she liked to sleep turned in my direction, where I could see her.

Was she doing it on my behalf? How often I'd wished for an invisible bridge between her room and mine—so I could slip into her bed, hold her until she fell asleep…or touch her until she moaned my name in pleasure. Dammit.

I shifted in my chair, uncomfortable, and she looked away from the window and back at me. She was just about to say something when the door to my office opened and my brother walked in with a scowl on his face.

"What the hell are you two up to?" he asked, looking back and forth between us.

I knew what he was thinking, and I could see the relief on his face when he saw that we were across the room from each other.

"I'm planning tomorrow's game, and your girlfriend is blowing up those balls over there." That sounded nasty, and I had meant it to.

Taylor looked over at Kam, who stiffened in her chair.

"Why the hell is she in here with you?" he asked me.

"Taylor..." Kam said, trying to stop him from overreacting.

"She's in trouble," I interrupted her, already sensing where my brother was going.

"Detention is supposed to be in the afternoon, when school is over," he grumbled.

"Tay, your brother changed it so I could go to work," Kam explained. That silenced him for a few seconds, but then he decided to challenge me further. "Fine. I want to do my detention in here, too."

I thought it over. True, I'd been dying to spend time alone with Kam, but I didn't know if I could control myself when I was alone with her, and considering the conversation we'd just had, I decided to play along.

"Fine, sounds good to me."

"What?" Kam said, perplexed. I was afraid she was giving us away.

"Something wrong?" Taylor asked, glaring at her. "You don't want me here?"

Kam fired back: "It's every free period for a month,

Taylor. I don't think it makes much sense for you to trade one afternoon in detention for a whole month here."

I couldn't tell if she didn't want to take the blame or if she wanted to be alone with me. He was outraged and turned to me: "A month?! What the fuck is your deal, Thiago? Don't you think we've been punished enough this year? You're my fucking brother! What's your goddamn problem with us?"

I didn't really know what to say, and before I could come up with something, the bell rang, ending our conversation. Kam walked over to Taylor and said, "Come on, I don't want to be late again," trying to pretend he and I weren't staring each other down.

"Thiago, let it go," Taylor said. "Enough with the games. I'm being serious."

"Fine. I'll let you off the hook, Kamila, if you promise not to do again what you did this morning."

She sounded angry when she said, dead serious, "I'd rather lose my free period than my freedom. I've got to go to class."

She walked past my brother and stomped off.

I looked down and shook my head.

She could be unbearable when she wanted to.

My brother walked up to me, looked me in the face, and said, "Stay away from her, Thiago, or I can't make you any promises."

He left before I could respond.

I felt guilty. And sad. And furious.

I wondered if Kam knew the effect she was having on us.

# CHAPTER FIVE

## Kami

THE GAME AGAINST ST. ANNE'S WAS THAT SATURDAY. I was excited, because I'd get to see Taylor play. Things hadn't been great between us, so going to his game seemed important, although Thiago would be there, too, and things with him were as bad as ever. Detention during my free period was tense and uncomfortable, and of course Taylor had insisted on joining me, so every day, for half an hour, the three of us sat there in near silence. It hurt to see them so distant. I couldn't help feeling like I was caught in the middle. Thiago hardly uttered a word to me, and Taylor just growled at him if he so much as tried.

Worst of all, the night before, after I got off work, I went over to their house to watch a movie with Taylor in his room. One thing had led to another, and we ended up having sex.

The problem was me, of course. I was physically there, in his bed, but my head was somewhere else. Taylor could tell I wasn't into it and lost his shit. He said he couldn't understand why I didn't want to, especially after it had been so long since the last time we'd done it. He accused me of turning colder and less caring by the day—while he hung on my every word.

I tried to tell him I was freaking out about everything: exams, work, Julian. My head was just somewhere else, but nothing I said seemed to matter; he was hurt and disappointed.

Things couldn't go on like this. We couldn't go on like this.

Thiago was right.

I needed to make a decision.

Ellie and I made plans to meet outside the coffee shop after I got off work so we could go to the game together. I changed my clothes, put on a bit of makeup, a wool hat, scarf, and my boots, and prepared us each a giant to-go cup of hot chocolate with Mrs. Mill's permission. It was technically still autumn, but as far as I was concerned, winter was upon us. Ellie was still a cheerleader, so she wore her uniform under a puffy coat, and she was perfectly made up, with her hair pulled back.

I was glad she hadn't quit the team. I enjoyed watching my friends cheer, even if I didn't feel drawn to it in the least. It had brought me much more misery than pleasure, and I liked who I was now.

Along the way, I brought back up the subject she hadn't wanted to talk about before: Was she really hung up on Taylor? And if not, why wouldn't she tell me who she liked?

"I need to know now, Ellie," I said for the fourth time

as we watched the people trickling into the gym. There were already parents in the stands. I wondered if Ms. Di Bianco would come.

Ellie sighed, and I could see her breath in the cold air. "First tell me what happened with Taylor."

"I don't know, Ellie. I'm feeling weird about it."

"Weird like what?" she asked. She glanced at the group of cheerleaders standing around chatting. I wasn't sure I should open up to Ellie about this, but she was my friend, and I had been planning on telling her about my feelings for Taylor and Thiago before I'd suspected she was in love with my boyfriend… Now I wasn't so sure…

"I'm confused," I continued. "I'm crazy about him, I really am, but…"

She gave me a look that left me speechless, and then her words left me cold, "…but you're even crazier about Thiago."

"What?!" I answered without thinking.

We stared at each other, saying nothing.

Was it really that obvious?

She knew. The look on her face gave her away.

"You can hide it from everybody else, Kami, but not from me." She looked almost disappointed as she said this. "Ever since the two of them moved back, you've been a completely different person. I get that your history left its mark, but I could tell from the beginning you were fixated on one of them. And it wasn't Taylor, Kami. It was Thiago."

"That's not true," I tried to argue, afraid someone would hear her and tell Taylor.

"Of course it is, Kami. And what I don't understand is why you're just playing with him the way you do."

"I'm not playing with anybody," I said, starting to feel flushed.

She groaned and dropped her arms in exasperation.

"Kami, just admit it!" she said, raising her voice, which startled me. "You don't feel the same way for Taylor that you do for Thiago, and he knows it. I'm sure he does!"

"You're wrong!" I retorted, my voice now on the rise as well. "The problem is that *you* like Taylor, and you're making all this up to confuse me!"

Ellie's eyes opened wide as she looked beside us, where suddenly Taylor had appeared out of nowhere. They both looked at me in shock. I closed my eyes and murmured, "Shit."

"You like me?" Taylor asked, incredulous and amused.

Ellie turned bright red and responded in an acid tone, "Not in your wildest dreams. The person you should be asking that question is Kami. Ask her who she's in love with. I bet you'll be surprised."

She walked over to the rest of the cheerleaders, who were waiting for her on the court.

Goddammit, Ellie.

Why did you do that to me?

Every ounce of amusement had disappeared from Taylor's face as if by magic, and I felt an ache in my chest.

"What was all that?" he asked. I'd never before wanted so badly to be able to read someone's mind and know what they were thinking. I tried to put up a wall so he couldn't see inside me, but I don't think it worked. When I didn't answer, he asked again, "Who are you in love with, Kami?"

I shook my head. "No one."

"I thought you'd say me," he replied, and I could see a deep sadness in his eyes, deeper than my own. A sadness accompanied by disappointment, anger, and a sense of betrayal.

"I do love you, Taylor," I said, and I wasn't lying.

"What was your best friend talking about, then?"

"I don't know. We were having an argument, and—"

Taylor interrupted me, taking my face in his hands. "Kami. I'm in love with you. Are you in love with me?" he asked calmly.

I hesitated as Thiago appeared in my line of sight, watching us from a distance. Did he wonder why I was crying? Could he see my tears from across the gym?

I shouldn't have looked at him. That was a mistake. Taylor turned to see what had distracted me, and all of a sudden, he understood everything. And so did I.

"I knew it," he said, looking down at the ground.

"Taylor, I—"

"Do you think I'm an idiot?"

"No, of course not!"

"I knew it," he said again. "I knew it wasn't just Thiago. I wanted to believe otherwise, that it was all on him, but I knew. Were you ever going to tell me? How long did you plan on lying to me?"

"I wasn't lying to you!" I said quickly, knowing that, too, was a lie.

When had I become such a horrible person?

"I've got to go warm up," he said, his voice so sad and dejected it broke my heart.

"Taylor, wait!"

"I've already waited too long."

I didn't see the look on his face when he said that because he was already on his way to the court. He knocked shoulders with Thiago as he walked past. Thiago looked at me, and I didn't know what to say.

Fortunately, not many people had seen; we didn't need to give them yet another reason to gossip. But then, in the end, it didn't matter, because Taylor made sure his name would be on everybody's lips that night.

The game started off as always, with Thiago telling our guys which plays to make before the two teams faced off. But Taylor was a disaster. He was distracted, the ref stacked him with several fouls, and when Thiago called time-out to talk to him, they started arguing.

Nobody understood what was going on. Thiago grabbed Taylor's arm and guided him away from the bleachers, but Taylor jerked away and shouted at him. At least the cheerleaders were in the middle of their routine. Between their chants and the music, nobody could hear what the two brothers were saying.

Then Taylor's arm flew out, and his fist struck his older brother's face. At that point, you could have heard a pin drop. I stood, as did many others, waiting on what was to come.

Thiago didn't move. He just touched his face and glowered.

"You're not going to do anything?" Taylor asked. We all listened attentively.

Instead of answering him, Thiago looked up at me, and I knew exactly what they'd been fighting about. Taylor followed his eyes and flew into a rage, pushing Thiago and nearly knocking him over. Members of the team stepped in to grab Taylor and separate the brothers, while Thiago stood there, calm and quiet—his expression impossible to decipher.

"You're my brother!" Taylor shouted. "How could you?!" His teammates dragged him off through the doors to the locker room, and once the other guys had come back, the game went on.

I knew what everyone expected me to do. And as Thiago turned his attention back to the court, acting as if nothing had happened, I didn't hesitate. Not because it was what was expected of me, not because it was the right thing to do, not even because it was my duty as his girlfriend. I did it because it mattered to me, *he* mattered to me, the guy who had been my companion on so many adventures, my playmate when we were kids, the guy who had protected me and made me laugh.

Taylor...

I couldn't hurt him.

I just couldn't.

I ran down the bleachers toward the locker rooms, passing Thiago, who grabbed my arm and stopped me. "What did you say to him?" he asked. The red mark on Thiago's cheek was already turning purple, and his eyes showed his sadness at having broken his brother's heart.

"Nothing," I told him, trying to break free. Being so close to him was the last thing I wanted. And at the same time, it was what I needed most. I was so plagued with guilt, smoldering inside me like hot embers, extending through my every cell... Burning, I was burning up. I attempted to pull away, but he held me fast.

"Don't go, Kamila," he pleaded. "It's not a good idea."

I freed myself. "What's not a good idea?" I asked. I knew it was selfish, that I shouldn't take it out on him, that he didn't deserve it, that neither he nor his brother had done anything wrong. It was me; it was my fault. I knew that I was projecting all the anger I felt toward myself on the one person I wanted to hurt least. "Don't touch me!" I yelled. "This is your fault!"

He was paralyzed. He let go of me as if my skin burned his hand and took a step back.

"You're confusing me! You always have!" I yelled.

Looking around, jaw clenched, Thiago said, "Kami, please, lower your voice." He was calm, and that made me realize I was making a scene with the whole school watching. And I realized if I mouthed off too much, Thiago's job could be in danger.

Stepping back, I said, "I'm sorry."

Just then, the audience roared, and Thiago glanced at the basket.

They'd just made a three-pointer.

I took advantage of his distraction and rushed into the locker rooms.

When I walked in, I didn't see him at first, and I thought he must have gone home. But then I heard the hissing of the showers in the back.

I approached slowly. And there he was. He still had his uniform on, but he was soaked from head to toe. His hair was dripping wet, plastered to his cheeks, and I could tell that he was crying.

I walked straight in and hugged him from behind.

He flinched, but he didn't push me away.

I pressed my cheek into his back and wrapped my arms around him.

How could I have ever hurt him?

The kindest person I'd ever known.

His hands met mine, and for a second I thought he wanted to hold me. I thought he'd embrace me and never let me go.

But no.

He peeled himself from my embrace and turned to look me in the face. That's when I knew I'd lost him forever.

"Do you love him?" he asked, his eyes fixed on me.

We were both sopping wet, our clothing soaked and dripping. It was way too cold to go outside like that, but all I could think was how the water was the only thing still holding us together.

Never in my life have I had to answer such a difficult question.

Did I love him?

I couldn't lie…

Of all the people in my life, Taylor was the one who

most deserved honesty from me. I forced myself to look him in the eyes, and I responded, "I love you both."

I could see the disappointment on his face—the grief—and I knew how selfish, how uncaring my response had been.

"That can only mean one thing," he replied. "You don't really love either of us."

He walked past me and out of the shower room, leaving me alone with my thoughts. Alone with my remorse. Alone with my sorrow. Sorrow over having lost him, because that's what his eyes had told me. I'd lost him…and I'd never get him back.

I'd have given anything to save Taylor from that pain, to make those last days as happy as the ones we had shared when we were first going out.

That would weigh on my conscience. But what I regretted most was not letting him know that he would have been the most sensible choice for me. The thing is, there's nothing sensible when it comes to matters of the heart.

# CHAPTER SIX

*Taylor*

I DRIED OFF, CHANGED CLOTHES, AND LEFT.

When had my life gone to hell? My brother and I were in love with the same girl, and not only had I lost my girlfriend, but I'd lost him, too, my partner, the guy who had been like a father to me.

Whatever.

It didn't matter anymore.

I was a wreck, and worse, there was something ugly growing inside me. And there was nothing I could do to control it. How could I ever lay eyes on my brother again when all I wanted to do was punch him in the face?

We couldn't live under the same roof now. Going on as if nothing had changed would be impossible. When I'd had a hunch that he might have a crush on her, it was different. I could still forgive him because he was my brother—but now?

I hadn't dared to ask Kami straight up. I couldn't bring myself to, because if I found out the two of them had done something, I'd kill him. My brother touching my girlfriend? He'd denied it, but Kami had confirmed that she loved him. She loved Thiago. I wished with all my heart it wasn't true.

Had they hooked up?

Of course they had.

How the hell else do you fall in love with a person?

Had I really been stupid enough to think Kami loved me? She said she loved both of us. No way. Bullshit! You can't be in love with two people at the same time!

As I walked to the parking lot, I was approached by the last person I felt like dealing with, given the circumstances. "What are you doing here?" I asked, reaching into my pocket for my keys.

"I just wanted to see how you're doing..." Ellie responded with her usual aloof coolness.

"Fucking fantastic," I replied coldly, walking past her to open the car door.

"I wanted to say I'm sorry," she said. That made me stop and turn.

"Sorry about what?" I asked, taking a closer look at her. Her hair was dark and wavy, pulled into two low pigtails tied with ribbons in the school colors. She was shivering from the cold despite wearing a winter coat and gloves, which made sense if all she had on underneath was her cheerleading uniform.

"About blabbing like that."

"At least you were honest. It seems everyone else was just lying to my face."

Ellie shifted uncomfortably from one foot to the other,

unsure what to say, then said, "Still, though, that was no way to find out. And it's not like I actually had any proof. It's just that I know Kamila, and…"

"Drop it," I cut her off. I hated people pitying me.

"Sure. Anyway, I'm sorry," she said. And I could tell that she meant it.

This was weird. Ellie had always been my girlfriend's friend. Not mine. She liked to tease me and get under my skin, but I never thought anything of it. Still, if what I'd heard on the bleachers was true, she liked me.

Really, though? Did Ellie really like me?

I tried to ask myself what I thought of her, which momentarily served as a good distraction from the hatred and sorrow I was feeling inside.

Ellie was pretty. Not too tall, slender but curvy. In the locker room, I'd hear guys talking about her ass, but I'd always ignored them. She had hazel eyes, long black lashes, and freckles all over her face.

She was the polar opposite of Kami…

And when I remembered that, I started hurting inside again.

"I need to go," I said, finally getting into the car.

"What about the game?" Ellie asked, her eyes full of worry. Was she worried about me? Or was she worried about the teammates I was leaving high and dry?

"Fuck it."

I turned the key and put it in reverse. When my headlights shone on Ellie, I took one last look at her. And then I saw him.

Yeah, him. Julian.

I jumped out of the car and ran like hell into the dark woods behind our school. Ellie was close behind me, trying to catch up, shouting, "What is it?"

"Come out, you son of a bitch!" I screamed, full of rage, hatred, and disgust. There was nothing I would have liked better than to grab hold of that bastard and beat him to a pulp.

"Who was it?" Ellie asked, panting as she caught up. But I didn't respond. We were both breathing hard as we turned on the flashlights on our cell phones.

"Be quiet," I told her, pricking up my ears. I was determined to find out where he was hiding.

He was still lurking around here. I knew it!

He wouldn't leave until he'd finished what he'd started. And his ultimate goal was to have Kami all to himself. That terrified me: the thought of him touching her, hurting her.

"Taylor, what are we doing here?" Ellie asked, grabbing my coat sleeve in fear.

"I saw Julian," I said, turning my head at the sound of a twig snapping.

"Julian!" she practically shouted, and I covered her mouth with my hand.

"Shhhh!" I said, flashing my cell phone in every direction, trying to see. I cursed as I realized he'd gotten away.

"Can we please get out of here?" she asked. Only then did I realize she was shivering. The poor thing was terrified. I took one more look around, but it dawned on me that staying there in the darkness with a psychopath on the loose probably wasn't the best idea. At least not with Ellie there. If I'd been alone, I wouldn't have cared.

"Let's go," I said, instinctively putting my arm around her to warm her up.

When we reached the school parking lot, people were already getting into their cars, and from the looks on their faces, I could tell we'd lost the game.

Great.

If we didn't win the next one, we'd be out of the semifinals. And even though I had a million other things going on in my head, basketball still mattered to me. A lot. And I had fucked up that night. I'd been off my game.

"I think we lost…" Ellie said when we reached my car.

"Yeah…" I said vaguely.

"Hey, Di Bianco! What the hell got into you?" a voice came from behind me. I turned and saw it was Victor.

I looked at Ellie and then back at him. All I wanted was to get the hell out of there, but I needed to warn Kami that I'd seen Julian. Just then, my brother came out of the gym. Even from afar, I could see the bruise on his cheek from where I'd punched him. I hadn't been able to help it, and as he caught sight of me, I asked myself how I would ever manage to forgive him for what he'd done to me.

"Shouldn't we call the cops? And let Kami know, too?" Ellie suggested.

I was tempted to say *screw that*, get in the car, and drive off—anywhere, it didn't matter, but I couldn't.

"We need to talk," Thiago said, walking up. When he noticed Ellie next to me, he added, "Alone."

"Cool, I'll see you," she said.

I pulled her closer to me and said, "You're not going anywhere."

Just then, Kami appeared a few feet away. Her hair was still wet from getting in the shower with me, and she looked utterly destroyed. My instincts told me to go to her, comfort her, do whatever I could to make her happy again, but that was no longer my role, and never would be again.

I looked at Thiago. "I saw Julian," I said, watching his body tense up as the words left my mouth.

"You did? Where?" he said, looking around, but the creep had undoubtedly taken off by then.

"In the woods," I said, pointing behind him.

He turned, and we both looked at Kami standing there. She seemed unsure what to do. Thiago asked what Julian had been doing, if we'd spoken to him, if he said anything. "No, he ran off," I responded.

"We've got to tell the cops," Thiago said.

I agreed. "Who's gonna go?" I asked. But I wanted to get the hell out of there, mostly because now Kami was heading over to us.

"Let's both go, Taylor," Thiago answered in a reconciliatory tone.

Just then Kami walked up and stood at his side, staring at me. "She's your responsibility now, bro," I spat. The words soothed my ego even as they pained my heart. "I'm going home," I added.

"Taylor, please," Kami said, her voice cracking as I walked to the car.

"Just forget we ever met, Kami," I answered. "You and I are done."

I thought Ellie might follow me, but a glance was all I needed to know she'd be staying behind with her friend.

Why should that surprise me?

Kami was the queen, and I would always be just another fool.

# CHAPTER SEVEN

*Kami*

HE WALKED OFF, AND I FELT A SINKING FEELING INSIDE, AS though part of me were leaving, too, an important part, one I couldn't do without, now gone forever.

But from the expression on his face, it was clear he'd made his choice, as much as it tore him up inside.

I looked at Ellie, who was also watching Taylor drive off, and I wondered what was going through her head. She seemed so sad when she turned to look at me.

"We saw Julian," she said. And those words were enough to pull me back to reality and everything I'd been trying to escape.

"What?" I asked, feeling the fear take over my body.

"My brother says they saw him in the woods, and then he took off running," Thiago explained.

I was unable to hold his gaze. Something inside me was broken, and being with him, even in public with my best friend, made me feel uncomfortable and incredibly guilty.

"I told you Julian was a coward," I said, clenching my jaw.

"Coward or not, we need to tell the cops," Thiago responded.

"Not to mention his parents," I said. Part of me thought that was more important, because scared as I was, his parents were probably worried about him, and they were the ones who could get him the help he needed. I was still struggling to understand how dangerous he could be and how serious his actions were.

"Fuck his parents," Thiago hissed. "Come on, I'll take you home," he said to me.

"No need," I replied, turning to Ellie. Was she aware of the consequences of what she'd blurted out earlier at the game? Had she done it on purpose to get closer to Taylor? To make the two of us break up? Staring at her in search of answers, I felt a new and very ugly feeling growing inside me. I didn't want to ask her for a ride because I didn't want to be around her, or around anyone. "I'll catch the bus," I told them.

Ellie's face showed she was hurt and even regretful. I was torn between anger and despair, and I needed to get out of there before I broke into tears. But as I turned to go, someone's hand caught me by the shoulder. "You're not taking the bus." Thiago was looking at me as if I'd lost my mind.

"Why not?"

"Do I honestly have to tell you?"

I knew he was right, but even though Julian wouldn't likely come at me on a bus full of people, I almost preferred risking an encounter with him than riding alone with Thiago.

"I'm gonna go with the girls," Ellie announced, taking

a step back. She looked like she wished she could just disappear. "Call you tomorrow, OK?" she said.

I didn't respond.

I was mad at her, mad at Taylor, mad at Thiago. Mad at the whole world, dammit! And you know why? Because sometimes, when you fuck things up, instead of reflecting on your actions and accepting the consequences, you end up taking out your frustrations on the people who care about you most.

I mean, how many times have you snapped at someone who's just asked how you're doing? How many times have you cursed everything and everyone else in the world when you're the one who did something wrong?

It's crazy the way the human brain works.

"Come on, I'll take you home," Thiago said, starting to walk over to his motorcycle. I hesitated, then followed him, realizing that if the two brothers had taken separate vehicles, things at home must have already been tense between them. Taking your motorcycle out for a spin in September was one thing, but riding it in this weather—that took commitment.

"You know I'm going to freeze to death on that thing," I snapped, mentally berating myself: *For God's sake, Kamila, it's not his fault! Not all of it, anyway!*

"Would you rather walk?" he retorted in a strained voice.

He handed me the black helmet he kept under the seat. I slipped it on, and it smelled like him. I couldn't help but inhale his scent; it was intoxicating.

He gently adjusted the strap for me, and my whole body stiffened when his fingers grazed the sensitive skin of my neck. Our eyes met, and I could tell he had noticed the way he affected me. But he didn't say anything except, "Let's go," before he got on the bike, releasing the kickstand and starting the motor, which roared so loud some of the nearby students turned to look.

Did Thiago realize they might think this was inappropriate? Was he worried about how it might affect his job?

I sat behind him and could feel his irritation when I gripped the handholds on the back seat instead of wrapping my arms around him, but he sped off so fast that all I could do was hold on tight.

The cold crept under the helmet, stung my face, and froze my fingers. That, and my fear as the speedometer kept climbing, made me forget any modesty or restraint, and I quickly changed my mind, holding on to him tight. I needed to feel safe and warm, to know he wouldn't let me fall.

It took a second before I realized he hadn't turned on the road that would lead us home, but instead was heading straight into town. "Thiago, where are we going?" I asked, but either he didn't hear me or else he just didn't want to answer.

When he parked in front of the police station, I said, "Why are we here?" I would have preferred to be anywhere else. I didn't want to talk about Julian. Especially not there. I didn't want to relive that awkward, shameful moment when my mother and I had to explain to the cops how Julian had taken a nude video of me and uploaded it to the internet.

"You don't have to go in with me," Thiago said. "You can wait out here; it's your call."

"There's no way I'm going in there," I told him as he got off the motorcycle, hanging the helmet from his left arm.

"No problem. Wait for me here, then."

He hurried inside before I could argue.

I looked around at the town I'd grown up in, asking myself when I had become the girl who gets harassed and stalked, who gets sneered at. The girl who gets dumped by her boyfriend because she hooked up with his brother.

I took out my phone and called Taylor. Don't ask me why. I just needed to hear his voice. I needed to say I was sorry; I needed to feel his arms around me.

Memories flooded my mind: our smiles and laughter as we goofed off in his room, his visits during my shifts at the café, cuddling on the couch watching movies. That was Taylor: the guy who could make you laugh, no matter what.

He didn't answer, so I hung up and looked at the photo of him on my home screen, blinking a tear from my eye. It rolled down my cheek, leaving a trail. I wiped it away with my forearm, trying to pretend I wasn't crying even though it was exactly what I deserved. I deserved to cry, to be alone, and as I told myself this, I kept staring at that photo from when I'd gone to decorate his house for Halloween. He had been coming up behind me in a Frankenstein mask, and I'd spotted him in the living room mirror, but decided to pretend I didn't know he was coming so I could scare him in turn.

I'd spun around and shouted "*Boo!*" He'd been so shocked, he'd fallen on the floor.

I couldn't stop laughing, and the look on his face had been so ridiculous, I just had to immortalize it with a photo. I'd pulled off his mask and given him a kiss on the cheek, and at the same time, taken a selfie of the two of us.

Even now, as stressed as I was, that photo still managed to make me smile.

"You can talk to him if you want, Kam," a voice behind me said.

I slipped my phone into my back pocket. I didn't respond, putting on my helmet, and asked Thiago, "Will you take me home now?"

It looked like he had something else to say, but he just said, "Hop on."

Again, he didn't take the road home, and I was surprised when I found us on a highway leading out of town. "Where are we going, Thiago?" I shouted over the rumbling of the bike. He said nothing, so I got more and more nervous, and soon we were in an empty field, all shadows except for his headlights. I saw trees left and right, and when Thiago stopped the bike and my eyes adjusted to the darkness, I noticed a boxy caravan parked there, and for a moment, my curiosity took over.

"What's that?" I asked as he killed the engine and the silence of the forest seemed to engulf us.

"Take off your helmet," Thiago said as he dismounted. I looked around. There was still a heavy layer of snow on the ground, and the trees were capped with white, their branches hanging low. In front of the camper was a circle of stones with ashes and burned logs in the middle. There must have been a fire there not long before.

"This is my new home," Thiago said.

"What?" I asked, shocked, stepping forward and walking around the caravan.

"I bought it a week ago," he said, stuffing his hands into his jacket. It certainly wasn't new, or even in decent condition, but I could imagine stepping out of it, looking up and gazing at the stars, or building a fire and sitting down to talk for hours.

I'd always fantasized about road-tripping cross-country in a camper like this. I'd asked my parents a million times if we could drive Route 66, but they'd never seemed interested. They were more the five-star-hotel types, even if every day was always the same at places like that. Luxury suites and fancy views got boring. The camper in front of me didn't look mobile, at least not in its current state, but I was curious to take a look inside.

"Why'd you bring me out here?" I asked him.

He shrugged. "We need to talk, right? And I figured this was a good place to do it."

"There's nothing to talk about," I said, sitting on one of the stones around the fire pit.

"Kam, my brother knows we have feelings for each other. Don't pretend like we can just ignore that."

I looked at a patch of trees as I buttoned my coat up and stuck my hands back in my pockets. It was freezing, but it felt good being out in the middle of nowhere. It was as if I was in another world, another time—somewhere I could think and reflect.

"What did they tell you at the police station?" I asked, trying to change the subject or at least buy a little time. I wasn't ready to face my feelings yet. And I sure wasn't ready to face Thiago's.

"They're a bunch of morons," he said as he walked around the side of the camper and came back with a few logs of firewood. "They said they'll let his parents know, but that's all they can do for now. For them, it's just a case of bullying, and they want the school to take care of it."

"How is the school going to deal with it? He's not even a student there anymore. They expelled him."

"I told them that," he said, arranging the logs and lighting a newspaper to get the fire started. Soon orange flames started to rise, and the pale, icy landscape around us took on warmer tones. I reached my hands out toward the bonfire, and soon the heat had warmed my bones. I felt good at last, and even better when Thiago went inside to make us a couple of cups of coffee, then came out and sat next to me. It was a subtle move, yet I couldn't help but notice he was finally trying to get close to me.

"Here," he said, handing me a mug. I cupped it in both hands and took a sip, feeling it warm me up on the inside.

"Thanks," I said, not taking my eyes off the fire.

"Kamila, I don't like this any more than you do, believe me," he confessed, and I could feel his eyes on me. I didn't turn, because I knew if I did, and I saw his face so close to mine, I would do something stupid, something that could only make things worse.

"He was my boyfriend. He was my best friend..." I said, already knowing how Thiago would respond.

"He *is* my brother," he affirmed, letting me know this was harder for him. He and Taylor were family.

"You think I don't know that?" I asked, my voice getting louder. I got up and walked away, hugging myself. "I'm the worst person in the fucking world!" I shouted to the trees. Feeling the chill in my bones, I walked back to the fire.

"Come here," Thiago said gently.

We were together. This was our chance—fleeting as it may be. There was no one on the other side of the door, no one about to arrive, no one to interrupt us, and being together was no longer forbidden. And yet, I told him, "I can't." I didn't even feel capable of looking him in the eyes. I covered my face with my hands and began to cry. I couldn't stop myself. I couldn't hold back. Not anymore.

For months, everything had been going wrong. Nothing had worked out. Everything I wanted to go one way inevitably went the other way.

Thiago hugged me from behind, and I melted into the soothing warmth of his big, strong arms.

His embrace.

What better shelter was there?

I turned around and hugged him tight, taking refuge in his body, letting him warm me up. It was just the two of us in this moment.

"There's nothing wrong with loving, Kamila," he whispered in my ear. "And that's something you're good at: loving. You wouldn't be in the position you're in if you didn't have so much love to give. Who can hold that against you?"

"It's wrong to love two people, though... It means there's something wrong with me."

He cupped my cheeks and lifted my face until I was looking him directly in the eyes. I had to blink a few times before I could see through my tears, but at last, when I focused on those bright-green eyes, I knew what he was saying was true.

Green eyes. Blue eyes.

I loved them both.

Was I in love with both of them?

"There's nothing wrong with you. You're just human," he said, wiping away my tears. "I'm only human, too, and I can tell you love is complicated. It's hard. You can love and hate someone at the same time. You can want them and wish you'd never see them again; you can be happy and sad at the same time; you can be furious and full of joy..."

I realized something right then.

Sure, you can love two people. But I only wanted to love one.

And that person was him.

I was absolutely certain of it.

He was the one who awakened things in me no one else could.

Thiago was the only one whose kisses made me want to

die, whose simple presence made me want to live... Fuck! Loving someone the way I loved him wasn't healthy, it wasn't good, not for me and surely not for him.

Could Thiago love me the way I needed? Could I give him the place in my heart he deserved?

"Spend the night with me, Kam," he asked me, and his lips grazed my cheeks, red from the cold. "Stay here, share the heat of your body with me, just give me that, and afterward, you can decide what you want to do... I promise I won't interfere... I won't tell you what to do, I'll accept whatever decision you make, but I deserve one night...just one night."

His request, and the things I saw in my mind when I imagined fulfilling it, made me nearly double over to try to calm the enormous butterflies in my stomach.

"Show me your new place," I said, gulping, my pulse racing.

What we would do in that caravan would mark a before and after. I knew that. We both did.

He let me go and led me inside. I felt as if I was entering directly into his mind, and I wondered how a person as mysterious as he was would decorate a home of his own, or this vehicle that was passing for a home. What I saw inside was the very last thing I would have imagined, knowing that it belonged to Thiago Di Bianco.

The furniture was rustic but cute. To the right, a table was wedged into a tiny space with a grayish sofa and blue plaid pillows. There was no way he'd bought those himself, and I was tempted to ask him where they'd come from.

The little kitchen had two small windows with curtains that matched the pillows. On the ground was an Iron Man doormat. He had obviously picked that out himself. Clean plates and glasses were piled up haphazardly in the drying rack. To the left was a double bed that just barely fit the space. It was neatly made, and a pile of books sat on a shelf that served as his nightstand. There was a TV in one corner, and another door that I guessed led to the bathroom.

I was surprised, as I walked farther in, to find the drawing I had made for him months before and that he had gotten so angry about. The image of us as kids with his sister, Lucy... It made my heart ache; I was touched.

This place, it was Thiago, it was everything he represented: austerity, gentleness, longing, masculinity, and most importantly, simplicity. Because that was what he was: a simple guy with small dreams, a brilliant mind, and a camper for a home.

That was him, and it wasn't surprising, exactly, because I had known all that already. What surprised me was how much I liked what I saw, and how I identified with all the little things there that were a part of him...and a part of me.

What surprised me was how much I felt at home.

# CHAPTER EIGHT

## Thiago

SEEING HER THERE—IN MY SPACE, WITH MY THINGS—IT did something to me. I wasn't proud of how that moment had finally come about, and I knew I had no right to expect anything. But I did. And whatever I was hoping for, it already had a bitter edge, because I knew it would hurt someone I loved more than myself. But we're all weak. Like I told Kami a few minutes before—we're only human.

I couldn't control what was going on in my body—or my head—every time I caught sight of her. I never could. Not when I was a kid and all I wanted was to get under her skin. And definitely not now, when just looking at her made me think about kissing her, holding her, having her beside me. Being her friend, her confidant, her lover. In my head, she'd always been mine—since that first, dumb kiss, back when I thought I knew what love was. There was a problem, though. She may have belonged to me in my mind—not like an object; I knew you could never possess another person. No, she belonged to me in a way that went beyond my own principles and prejudices. My soul cried out for her, my heart needed her, my body longed for her every single day.

I was in love.

A person knows these things, and if you aren't sure, it means something is wrong. And that was what got to me: I was scared of taking a wrong step. Kam had feelings for my brother. She had to. She was crying over him. Missing him.

Is it true that you can love more than one person? I couldn't wrap my head around that, but maybe that was me, maybe I was too uptight, too old-fashioned, maybe I didn't understand those kinds of feelings because I couldn't imagine loving anyone but her.

I couldn't judge her—human minds are too complicated for that—but still, every tear she shed for my brother broke my heart.

Was I jealous?

I didn't know, but what I felt when I saw her with him or imagined them together was an ugly feeling, one I wasn't proud of and didn't want to harbor.

It was difficult—all of it—because I understood how she could love Taylor. He was incredible. Who the hell wouldn't love him?

What I didn't understand was why she was in love with me.

Did that even matter? Did I need to understand it? Did I care? Because she was there, right? And the way her body reacted when I was near had to mean something—something serious, something important. Didn't it?

"Who picked out those cushions?" she asked.

Like always, she caught me off guard. I blinked, confused at first, until I realized what she was talking about.

"Those? They were in here when I bought it," I answered, studying her profile, her little nose. I'd always liked the shape of it. Especially because it was so expressive. You're probably wondering how a person can use their nose to express anything. Kamila Hamilton could. It would wrinkle when something grossed her out, and twist slightly when she was deep in thought. When she smiled, it would turn upward, and when she got impatient, her nostrils would flare. And then there were her eyes: rich brown and expressive, framed by a precious halo of eyelashes. I was always struck by her combination of light skin, blond hair, and heavy dark lashes. When she looked at me, it transported me elsewhere. She could drive me crazy, and she could reel me back in. One look and I was willing to do anything, anything, just to be the center of her universe.

"I figured," she remarked, making her way farther inside.

She stopped close to my bed—too close. Not on purpose, and it's not like there was anywhere else to go, the place was pretty small, but once I saw her there, my mind flooded with the possibilities.

How many times had I imagined undressing her—slowly, carefully, taking my time to kiss every inch of skin, all the spots no one else would think to touch? Or just the opposite—rushed, rough, desperate, like I couldn't get close to her fast enough. People say we're just animals, all instinct. And maybe that's true. I was trying to keep mine in check. But some days, it felt impossible.

Did she feel the same thing when she saw me? Did she want to tear my clothes off and kiss me all over?

I turned away with the excuse of switching the heater on, hoping to give myself a moment to calm down.

"I like it," Kam said, and I looked back at her. That smile, those eyes still red from crying, that blond hair tousled from the motorcycle ride. Every bit of her moved me in a way I still couldn't express in words.

She was gorgeous, magnificent, the sweetest person in the world. She was the girl of my dreams.

"I like *you*," I couldn't help but respond, and I watched her absorb those words.

"I don't understand why," she said.

Shaking my head, I replied, "If only you could be in my head right now. Because I promise you every one of your doubts would vanish." I took a step toward her.

She looked out the window and remarked that it was snowing. I looked to see the flakes gently falling. And that made me realize something.

"It would be dangerous to drive you home," I said, taking a step closer.

"Because of the snow?" she asked.

"The motorcycle could skid, especially if the road's iced over. I wouldn't want to put you in danger."

"I'll call my mom and tell her..." The way she hesitated made me even crazier about her.

"That you won't be coming home tonight?" I could

tell her heart was beating faster. I could feel mine doing the same. Was she frightened?

"But you'll take me if it stops, right?" she asked.

"I'll take you wherever you want, whenever you want. Just say the word."

I had to remember she was younger than me... Maybe she didn't want to spend the night. Maybe it didn't feel as urgent to her as it did to me now, as I could feel myself getting hard.

But my words seemed to relax her. I couldn't help but try to remind myself: *Relax, Thiago! Don't fuck this up.* "You want some macaroni and cheese?" I asked, turning on my tiny stove.

"Sure," she responded, flopping down on the couch. As I started taking ingredients out of the fridge, she asked, "Do you know how to cook?"

Offended, I replied, "I've been cooking since I was thirteen." I put on water to boil.

"If you think you can cook, then I should be on *Top Chef*," she replied, standing and rolling up her sleeves. "I can promise you, you've never tasted macaroni and cheese like mine."

Resting my hips against the counter, I said, "Don't underestimate my culinary abilities."

"Don't underestimate mine."

She was so much shorter than me that I had to look down, and it was hard to resist the urge to grab the back of her neck and pull her in for a kiss. She must have known that's what I wanted, but I could tell it wasn't the right time, so I smiled at her, and we got to work. It was amazing to be together like that, alone, at ease, without having to worry someone might interrupt us, knowing we were doing nothing wrong. After all, my brother now knew about us, so we weren't lying anymore. I didn't have anything to feel bad about, right?

I was kidding myself. I knew that. Making excuses to keep from feeling like an asshole. But I needed this. I needed this moment of intimacy with Kam. As for the guilt, the consequences—I'd deal with them tomorrow.

I put on some music, and we had dinner at the little table beside the sofa. I wasn't ashamed of the place, but I was anxious to know what she thought of it, to see how she'd feel in that small space and to find out if our lives were really as incompatible as I'd always feared.

But they weren't. Not at all. Kam even slipped off her boots and sat on her knees on the sofa, spooning big bites of macaroni and cheese as she told me all about her interview at Yale in a few months.

Another thorn in my side, because it reminded me that she would be leaving. She'd be gone, dammit. And there I'd be living in a piece-of-shit caravan. It wasn't much, but it gave me my own private space.

There was one thing, though: I hadn't told Mom yet. Taylor didn't know anything, either. And I had the feeling that I should keep it a secret for now.

"Since when are you into campers?" Kam asked, finishing her plate and setting it on the counter.

"I've always kind of wanted one," I said, cleaning up

what little there was—just the dishes, one glass, and one empty bottle of beer. "I'd been considering getting one for a while; rent costs a fortune, and it's not like the school pays me that well…"

"I love it!" she exclaimed, interrupting me. "It's so homey, and it's so…you!"

"Yeah. Wait till the first time you get up in the morning and you find a field mouse in the toilet."

Kam hugged her legs and squirmed, looking all around, which made me laugh.

"Relax," I said, "I've got the situation under control." That was true. But the first night I'd spent here, I wouldn't have wished on anyone.

"What does your mom think? And…" I knew she was going to say *Tay*, but she stopped herself.

"They don't know," I replied, sitting back on the sofa. She had made a little hollow there for herself, settling in against the wall. I wanted to get close and kiss her. But I went on, "With Taylor going to college next year, I'm kind of worried about leaving her alone. I might just kind of come and go and maybe not fully move out."

"Wow," Kam said. "That's so sweet of you. A lot of guys would just move out, period." She looked almost proud of me.

"Well, I'll probably spend some more time out here for now, since things between Taylor and me are so tense, and I know Mom has been worried about that."

Kam looked down, realizing my not-so-subtle way of bringing up the topic we really needed to talk about.

"Your brother will never forgive me for this," she said.

"What do you mean by *this*?" I asked.

"What I feel for you…"

"He's going to have to learn to live with it, Kam. I've had to live with knowing you love him. Knowing you've kissed him, that you've had sex with him."

She closed her eyes and wrapped her arms around herself. Then she said, "Can I confess something to you?"

I nodded and waited.

"It never felt right."

"What didn't?" I couldn't help but ask.

"The sex…" Her cheeks blushed a beautiful pink as she said this. "It felt like…like…"

"Like what?"

Her hesitation told me that she knew what she was about to say would mark our destinies.

"Like I was doing something wrong," she said.

I shook my head. I'm not sure why, but I think it was because I'd been hoping she'd say something else— something about me. I tried to push that feeling aside with a joke: "Don't tell me you felt like you were doing something sinful!"

She grinned briefly and said, "No. I felt like I was cheating on you."

I held my breath. She covered her face with her hands and squealed, "I know! It's ridiculous!"

Feeling an inner peace I hadn't experienced for a long time, I grabbed her by the hands and told her, "No. No, it isn't. It can't be. Because I've felt the same way…with every girl I've slept with, Kam. You left your mark on me. It's just that I was too young to know back then that I had already met the love of my life."

"But, Thiago, that's crazy, that's…"

"It's my truth," I interrupted her, bringing her hands to my lips and kissing her knuckles. "And it can be yours, too, if you want."

The seconds before she spoke were some of the most uncertain I'd ever felt.

# CHAPTER NINE

## *Kami*

THERE WE WERE—TRULY ALONE FOR THE FIRST TIME SINCE Thiago came back to Carsville. Not in a car, not at school. No distractions. No excuses. Just us.

How can I explain how I felt sharing this moment with Thiago Di Bianco? Can you even imagine it? Just watching him cook made my thighs clench and my heart race like it was about to give out.

He was so sexy, so big and manly moving around in that tiny, cozy space. Everything he did fascinated me. My eyes followed his enormous hands as they held on to the colander or opened a beer. Everything he did turned me on, waking me from a sexual lethargy I hadn't realized I'd been in until this last half hour alone together, culminating with him telling me I was the love of his life.

He wasn't lying to me, was he?

No, he wouldn't lie to me about something like that. But it was so crazy, so unreal, the thought that he had felt so strongly about me ever since we were kids. Why should it surprise me, though? I'd felt the same way about him. It was as if there were a cord pulling me toward him.

Have you heard of the red thread of fate? That tale about how we're destined to meet someone who will be the love of our lives? It might sound ridiculous, but I knew my feelings for Thiago surpassed anything I could have felt for Taylor or Danny or any other guy. With Thiago, things were just different.

I'm not saying the red thread legend is real, but maybe, just maybe, we were meant to be together.

"It's funny because none of this seems real," I said as he kissed my knuckles.

"We don't choose who we love," he said, looking at me the way every woman should be gazed upon at least once in her life.

"Do we choose who we fall in love with, though?" I asked.

He smiled, and the world spun around me faster and faster as he responded with a question: "Does that mean you're in love with me?" He was trying to be clever.

"All I know is I know nothing," I replied.

"Are you quoting Socrates to me?" he asked.

"Would you prefer someone else?"

"How about instead of talking, you put those lips to better use?"

We looked at each other, and the world seemed to stop. It wasn't a passionate kiss. It wasn't showy. It began with a simple caress on the cheek before he wove his fingers into my hair, pulling me close and pressing his lips to mine.

For a moment, things felt strange, as if we'd been blind and could now see for the first time, or as if our hands had been covered by gloves that had just been removed, and we could finally feel each other's skin without anything coming between us.

I felt guilty, because I knew those blinders and gloves were more than metaphorical. They had a single, very concrete name: Taylor.

He had kept us apart. Well, not him, but me, because I was the one responsible, I was the one who had liked him, sought him out and agreed to be in a relationship with him. But the whole time, just as in the legend, I had felt the pull of the red thread that tied me to my soulmate, tugging persistently.

"Come here," he whispered, wrapping me in his huge arms and positioning me on top of him. There was hardly space, but that didn't stop him, and soon he kicked the table back so he could kiss me the way he wanted.

His tongue in my mouth again after so long was a revelation. His scent filled the room, permeating everything. His massive hands moved up my back as I stroked his face. I couldn't get enough of his stubbly skin, and I kept blinking to convince myself this was real.

We stopped kissing for a moment, but only to meet each other's eyes, communicating things that were impossible to say with words—things we didn't fully understand, and yet were so meaningful now, after all this time. Without a word, he picked me up and carried me to his bed. I let him. I knew he wanted me, and I wanted him.

We deserved that moment, just the two of us. We deserved that intimacy to step into a timeless space where no one and nothing could interrupt us.

Feeling his weight against me, the only thing I thought was, *I'm home.*

I belonged to that moment, to that place... To hell with the consequences, to hell with remorse, to hell with whatever I'd have to deal with later!

Something inside me needed to hold him tightly and never let him go, urging me to take advantage of every instant we could devote to our pleasure, letting our bodies speak to each other in ways that words failed to do.

He slipped his hand under my T-shirt, tracing intricate patterns on my skin, tickling me. "What are you doing?" I asked, giggling.

Thiago smiled, and I thought I would faint.

What was it about this boy that drove me so insane?

*He hardly ever smiles*, a voice inside said. The rarer something is, the more you appreciate it.

"I have a few reservations," Thiago said suddenly, looking to me for the answers.

"About what?"

"I don't want to screw things up with you... I don't want to rush it. We don't have to do this now, we can wait and see how things go, how you end up feeling about Taylor..." I put my hand over his lips, not wanting his brother to cast a shadow over this moment.

"Shh," I said, pulling him close. "Whatever you have to tell me, tell me with kisses."

And that's what he did.

He kissed me and… My God, what a good kisser!

He took his time—I remembered he'd always been that way. Even when we were little and got candy, Thiago would always save some for later, while Taylor and I would pig out.

*You've got to dose it out*, he used to say, and he would nibble his chocolate or lick his lollipop slowly. Sometimes he'd even wrap it back up and save it for later. *That's how you make it last*, he'd say.

And that was how he did it with me.

And it drove me wild.

His mouth toyed with me, his hands undressed me, so slowly it felt like sweet torture.

I tried to tear off his clothes, I wanted a glimpse of his sculptured body, I wanted to kiss him all over, but he wouldn't let me. He held my wrists with one hand while the other peeled away each of my layers, licking, biting, and kissing every last corner of my body.

Fully realizing where he was headed, I felt shy and hesitant, but at the same time, I was eager.

He started gently, kissing around me, getting closer, making me throb with pleasure. Then he reached my center and licked and kissed. I could feel his hot breath, and I thought I would literally die from it all. He was savoring me as if I were the most delicious fruit.

"I could stay here all night," he whispered into me, taking me to the edge of orgasm. "Not yet," he said, sitting back and pressing me into the mattress.

Outside, the snow had turned to rain, and the pitter-patter against the tin roof created an absurdly romantic mood inside the caravan. I never wanted to leave.

"Not yet?" I asked.

Did he know what he was doing to me? That he had transported me to another universe? Did he know how hard it was for me to even get there—how much it meant to be pushed that close to climax, only for it to slip away?

"You'll come when I tell you to," he said. I was so turned on by those words that when his tongue touched my clit again, it was like a bomb going off. Neither of us expected that, and once my scream had ended—that was the first time I'd ever come so hard, so it had been impossible not to scream—I felt as though something long trapped inside me had finally been set free. It set Thiago free as well. His reserve was gone—he was no longer the guy who saved his candy for later—no, he wanted something, and I could tell he wanted it now.

"I can't believe you came," he said in a gruff voice, not so much angry as frustrated. Meanwhile, he kept tearing off more layers of my clothing.

"Jesus, you're like an onion," he said, making me laugh as he stripped off my undershirt, then he pressed his palm into my lips and confessed, "I need to fuck you, Kam." This wasn't anything to laugh at. He continued: "I need to fuck you for hours. Once or twice won't be enough…"

"You're ambitious," I told him, feeling around for his erection and giving it a squeeze.

My God, he was so hard…

Now I was the one in control. He let me take over, and I moved slowly down until my mouth was nearly touching the tip. Then I licked, nibbled, kissed—I was trying to replicate what he'd done to me. But in seconds, he had sat upright, and with a wild look in his eyes, he commanded me, "Put it in your mouth."

I didn't hesitate. I was happy to do it. I had never been one to save anything for later.

I sucked on him as long as I could, bringing him to the verge of orgasm, but I knew if we went on like that, we'd never get around to the main event, and I needed to feel him inside me.

"I can't take it anymore," he said, reaching over to the nightstand and grabbing a condom, which I watched him slip on. I lay back, waiting for him to lay on top of me, but he surprised me by saying, "Get on all fours."

I started to sit up, but he couldn't wait, and he grabbed my waist and pulled me backward. I'd never done it that way, and I knew it would be new and different. Especially with him, because he was older, because he had experience, and because he had awakened something inside me no one ever had before: a hunger, an urge to feel pleasure with every fiber of my being.

When Danny and I had done it, it had been a disaster. With Taylor it had been nice, slow, pretty, romantic, but even then, I can't say I was satisfied.

Thiago, though—he drove me crazy. He revealed a part of me I hadn't known existed. And I can't tell you how liberating it was.

We didn't just do it once. We didn't just do it twice. We did it over and over, sometimes slowly, whispering in each other's ears—profound things, sweet and glittery, sometimes even funny. We did it fast, too, talking dirty, whispering naughty words to each other. We let out everything we'd held back for months.

———

I don't know when I fell asleep, I just know that when I opened my eyes the next morning, the sun was bright and shining through the thin checkered curtains on the windows. I reached out to turn off the alarm on my cell phone and felt someone groaning under me, trying to wake. I looked down to see Thiago's eyes, Thiago's smile, the most handsome smile I'd ever seen.

I don't know how, but I'd fallen asleep on top of him, naked.

I felt myself getting hot with embarrassment, and I pulled away, but he grabbed me in what felt like a jujitsu hold, and I couldn't escape.

"Where do you think you're going?" he asked, pressing his nose into my neck and pulling me onto his blazing-hot bare body.

I didn't answer, I just kissed his neck, wondering if I would be able to keep enjoying this incredible experience or if the day would bring me back to my problems.

My phone dinged and dinged as messages came in. Some of them, I knew, would be from my mother.

"I need to go home," I said, but Thiago gripped me tight.

"*This* is your home," he said as I struggled to reach to my phone.

"Calling this a home is a bit of an exaggeration, no?" I quipped. I loved the way he just shrugged. Appearances didn't matter to Thiago. He didn't care what other people thought.

"You make it feel like an oasis," he replied, kissing me on the tip of my nose.

"I was kidding," I told him, "I love it here." I reached up and stroked his hair. I'd wanted to do that so many times. Finally, I could.

"Who'd have thought?" Thiago said, musing to himself. "Compared to your house, I mean…"

Smirking, I said, "Yeah, like your mom's place is a shack."

He laughed. "You know your house is the fanciest one in the neighborhood. Everyone else is just trying to keep up."

"I'd say they're doing a pretty good job," I said. "Speaking of, doesn't it scare you, being out here alone?" I wouldn't have lasted a second sleeping out there by myself.

"What would I be scared of? Wolves?"

Terrified, looking out the window, I asked, "Are there wolves out here?"

"We're on the edge of a forest. It's not likely they'd come close to us, but yeah, there are wolves." He stopped talking and nibbled on my ear.

"Do you really think a wild animal could come after us?" I asked, returning to the subject.

"The only animals I'm worried about are human beings," he said, standing up and leaving me there, naked and cold.

"You know this conversation is scaring the shit out of me?"

He grinned and took a frying pan out from a small drawer under the sink. "If you're with me, nothing bad will happen to you, I promise you that. Now, are you in the mood for pancakes?"

I nodded, feeling around in the sheets for my underwear and bra and put them on, not wanting to walk around naked.

Suddenly something soft hit me on the head. I lifted it off and saw it was one of his T-shirts.

"Throw that on," he said, and as I did, I felt like a fan at a concert when the singer touches their hand. Was I that hung up on him? He looked at me with lust in his eyes, grinned, and said, "It looks good on you."

"And you look good without it," I told him, gawking at his abs and chiseled body.

"Yeah?" he said, taking out the ingredients for the batter.

"Let me help you," I said, standing next to him and watching his every move. I couldn't help it. I loved being in the kitchen, I was good at cooking, and it was hard for me to give up control.

The two of us cooked in comfortable silence, and I couldn't help remembering the day Taylor and I had made pancakes at his house. He had no idea what he was doing, and all he did was get in the way and mess everything up.

We even got in a food fight, throwing flour and batter all over each other until we were both lying on the floor with a mess all around us. I thought his mother would kill us when she saw the kitchen. That made me realize how different the two brothers were. Thiago was meticulous, a perfectionist, but I missed Taylor's spark, which came across no matter who he was with. I had to understand something, though. I couldn't have both of them, I couldn't mix them together in a test tube and create the perfect guy. The perfect guy didn't exist, and the sooner I admitted to myself that Taylor was gone for good, the better.

Thiago set the table while I made coffee. Then we sat down for breakfast.

"How are we going to handle things at school today?" he asked.

"Handle what?" I asked, wiping my mouth with a paper towel.

"We both need to go, but we shouldn't be seen arriving together. I think we should wait for everything to settle and for my brother to get used to the idea of…"

"Of us?" I asked.

Thiago reached up and pinched my earlobe. "You know nobody can know about us, right?"

I nodded.

It wouldn't be a good look, to say the least. They'd probably fire him if they found out.

"We'll see each other here, when we can, okay?" he said. That reassuring look on his face made all my doubts melt away.

I wished I could hide out there forever, but I had class.

Even today, I still ask myself what would have happened if we had decided to skip that day and stay there.

Things happen for a reason, I'm sure of that. Life takes twists and turns like a roller coaster, and you never know when the ride will end. Or maybe you never get off.

We tidied up quickly, showered together in the tiny bathroom, stole a few more kisses and enough caresses to keep our bodies burning inside for the rest of the day, before we had to call it quits. It was time to go.

Outside, it was snowy, and it was hard to get the motorcycle started.

By seven thirty, Thiago was dropping me off at home. I looked over at his mother's house and prayed Taylor couldn't see us.

"Kiss me," he said, putting a hand on the back of my neck and drawing me in.

One more kiss and a few sweet words, and then we parted ways.

If I had known what lay in store for us that day, there are a thousand other things I would have said. I would have drawn that moment out for the rest of my life.

# CHAPTER TEN

## *Taylor*

I SAW THEM ARRIVE. I SAW THEM, BUT I WASN'T STUPID enough to let them see me.

It hurt. It sure as fuck did. It hurt and made me angry. And the anger felt better than the hurt. I preferred the rage a thousand times more than that deep, awful pain that left me feeling shattered.

Kami's betrayal was something I could never forgive, but my brother's? That was worse. For me, our relationship was over.

I had no idea where they were coming from—a hotel? But one thing was obvious: They had spent the night together. And I couldn't stop asking why. Didn't Kami feel our connection when we were together? I always felt it when I was near her.

She turned toward her front door, but then she stopped and smiled at him one more time.

At him. At him, dammit.

I looked away from the window and finished getting dressed. I dreaded going to school, and I even thought about playing sick, staying home to avoid the situation. But exams had begun, and I had math that day, and I'd need to nail it if I wanted to get into my top picks for college.

I was pulling a Knicks sweatshirt over my head when my phone buzzed.

I had ignored Kami's calls and messages, but then when she stopped, I was disappointed. I wanted to hear from her own lips that she was sorry, that she'd made a mistake. But of course, that didn't happen. She'd just quit trying, and I'd sat there staring at the ceiling, trying to absorb the fact that my girlfriend was in love with my brother.

But now I saw her name on my screen again, and I wasn't sure what to do.

I didn't want to talk to her, I couldn't, not after seeing her pull up on my brother's bike. I read her text message:

> I know I'm the last person you want to hear from right now, but please, please forgive me, and don't hate Thiago. I love you, and I hope when you're ready you'll let me talk to you and explain everything.

What was there to explain? That she'd cheated on me? Fooled me? To hell with that! And as for not hating my brother, who was she to ask that of me? How could she dare get mixed up in my business?

I was pissed. Furious.

I grabbed the car keys and hurried downstairs, hoping to get out of the house without seeing my mother, but as I walked through the kitchen, there she was, and worse, so was Thiago. Mom could tell something was off when Thiago saw me and the atmosphere became so tense that it felt electric.

"I'm going to grab breakfast on the way," I said, trying to get out the door.

"Why? What happened now?" my mother asked, looking back and forth between us.

"Taylor, we need to talk," Thiago said.

"About what?" I asked, my hand on the doorknob. "About how you're fucking my girlfriend?" My mother looked shocked. She scolded me for cursing, but I didn't care. What really got to me was the look on Thiago's face.

So I was right. They had done it. I didn't need proof, I didn't need him to admit it aloud. One look told me it was true.

"You fucker," I hissed, scowling at him in a way I don't think I ever had before.

"Taylor!" my mother shouted, angry and tense. I felt betrayed. I hated every cell in his body right then.

"You can't talk that way in front of Mom," Thiago said, standing. "Tell her you're sorry."

I laughed. "You honestly think you have the right to tell me what I can and can't say after what you've done?"

"Whatever you have to say to me, you can say it in private, not in front of her," he replied.

"Sorry, Mom," I said, not feeling it in the least. My fists were clenched so tight I thought my nails would cut into my palms. "I'm sorry you raised a son who's a lying, manipulative narcissist."

"Thiago, what did you do?" my mother asked, looking him straight in the eyes as he glared at me.

"Is that what you really think?" Thiago said.

I didn't hesitate: "Yes, I think that, because it's the truth. You think everyone and everything revolves around you. Kami was my girlfriend, and you had no right to come between us."

"Let me tell you one thing, Taylor," he fired back, maintaining his composure, as he always did in these moments—that was something that drove me crazy about him. "I'm sorry for what happened with Kam, and I never wanted things to go this far. I tried to stay away. But we can't control who we love. And I've loved her since I was ten years old."

"She was mine," I shouted, clenching my jaw. Then his face transformed, and he reached up and grabbed the collar of my shirt.

"She belongs to no one."

I pushed him backward. "Don't you dare put your hands on me."

"Or what?"

"Enough!" my mother shouted. "You're brothers! You can't let a girl come between you; family's more important than that…"

"Oh, please. Don't come at me talking about family…" I responded.

"Mom's right," Thiago said. "I didn't make all these sacrifices so we could end up like this." He ran his hands down his face.

"You and your fucking sacrifices… You're not the only one who's had to make sacrifices, Thiago!" I shouted.

"Everything I've ever done, I did so you and Mom wouldn't want for anything," he said, looking wounded. All I saw was hostility, lies, and more lies. I was blind with rage, and I couldn't see the truth in any of what he was saying. "I gave up everything so you could go to a good school and be captain of the basketball team; I coached you so you could make it to the finals…"

"Excuse me," I intervened, "but I'm the one who's spent hours bent over the books studying and even more hours at the gym. You didn't do anything for me. I did it all myself."

"If it wasn't for Mom and me, you would've had to drop out of school and work," he said.

"Are you going to hold that against me? Dad offered us child support! You're the one who turned it down! You're the one who said we didn't need it!"

"You want his fucking blood money?" he asked.

"Thiago!" Mom and I shouted at the same time.

I continued: "He didn't kill her! He may have been a cheating bastard, he may have been an asshole, but he didn't kill her, dammit! It was an accident!"

My brother transformed. That was no surprise. The subject of our sister was off-limits. The mere mention of her was enough for my mother to bury her face in her hands and burst into tears.

"His mistakes are what killed her, and for me, that makes him a murderer, a murderer who ruined my life and took away all my opportunities—like the ones you have right now," Thiago said.

"You're not the only one who lost a sister and a father, Thiago. You keep talking about my opportunities. Well, I fought for them! You picked the easy path, and look how it turned out! And now you're so jealous of me that you couldn't help but steal the girl I love right out from under me! Well, go on! Go live your life and leave everyone else in peace!"

Thiago went quiet and looked at me—long enough that I couldn't tell if it was minutes or hours. Then he turned to Mom, who was sitting in a chair, crying.

She'd never seen us argue like that before. What was happening to us?

"Taylor, I never intended to take anything from you," Thiago said softly. He looked tired now, and much older than he really was, and a tiny part of me, deep inside, felt sorry for him. "If this is what you really think, then it means I didn't do as good a job as I thought. And if you ask me to stop seeing her, then I will. You're my brother, and I love you. I lost a sister, I'm not going to lose you, too. But I love her. I'm in love with her. Do you really want me to stay away?"

He had looked me in the eyes, wanting me to see that he was sincere. I didn't need to think it over. "Yeah. I want you to stay away from her. And from me. Forever."

# CHAPTER ELEVEN

## Kami

MY MOTHER TOOK MY BROTHER AND ME TO SCHOOL. After what had happened with Momo and Julian and Cam's classmates, he was no longer the same kid. He still ran around the house dressed up as a caterpillar, a spider, or some monster, holding his iguana Juana in one hand and his laser pistol in the other, but something about him had changed. He was more skittish, more dependent, and way more insecure than he'd been before they'd bullied him.

Kids can be cruel, and I knew firsthand how bad the consequences of someone mistreating you could be.

"Should I pick you up, or is Taylor coming to get you?" my mother asked as we pulled up to school and got out. I was buttoning my brother's coat and pushing a wool hat down onto his head.

"Taylor told me he'd take me to the go-cart track this weekend," my brother said with excitement in his little blue eyes.

It had been a miracle getting my mother to accept my relationship with the son of the woman whose marriage she had destroyed, but she'd gone beyond that, and it was proof that she'd really changed. How, then, could I turn around and tell her Taylor and I had broken up? And how would she react when I started going out with Thiago? Even I couldn't admit to myself what was going on with Thiago. I knew it would be a long time before either of our families would accept that we loved each other.

How naive I was then, worrying about that, with no idea of what lay in store.

"Why don't you pick me up?" I said, focusing my eyes on my brother. I didn't want her to suspect anything, to get nosy and start asking questions.

"OK, see you guys later," she said, kissing my brother and giving me an inquisitive glance.

I grabbed Cameron's hand and started walking him toward the building.

"Hey, Kami," he said, scratching his forehead and all but removing his hat, "is it true that Momo was just your friend in disguise?"

I wondered where that question was coming from. We had talked a long time about how Momo didn't exist and no one was going to hurt him.

"He's not my friend anymore, Cameron," I answered, looking around. The thought of seeing Taylor or Thiago made me nervous. I didn't know what Taylor would do or say after what had happened the day before, and I didn't know how I'd resist throwing myself into Thiago's arms to be enveloped by his scent.

I hadn't been able to stop thinking about him, going

back over the night we'd spent together. His hands, his mouth, his body against mine, our passion, comfort, and pleasure. I'd never known anything like it.

What would he do when he saw me?

I knew we needed to keep what we'd done secret, at least for a while, but what I hadn't expected was that he would pass me by without so much as a glance. I was left staring at him as he continued down the hall. I told myself this was part of the plan. That this was how we would keep it secret from the students, the teachers, the principal, and the rumor mill.

But when Taylor saw me, it was totally different. He didn't duck me, didn't avoid my gaze, he just stopped to say hi to my brother.

"What's up, champ?" he said as Cam looked at him, bright-eyed. "You ready for our big hang tomorrow night?"

I could tell that, though he was trying to hide it, pain was consuming him from within. So why was he trying to pretend otherwise?

"Listen, Taylor," I began, but Cam screamed over me: "Yessss!!"

"Cool, see you later, kid," he said, pulling off his hat and giving his hair a tussle. Then, when I thought he would leave without uttering a word to me, he asked, "Can we talk at lunchtime?"

"Sure," I responded, a little confused, and he bent down and gave me a peck on the cheek.

What the hell was going on?

"Come on, Cam," I said.

I had to leave my phone in a plastic bag as I walked in the building, same as every day. After what had happened with Julian, they were taking their anti-bullying measures seriously, and there was a zero-tolerance policy for phones during school hours. When I was done, I walked Cam to his classroom. "See you later, OK, buddy?" I said, giving him a kiss on the cheek.

"Hey, Kami? What if we just went back home?" he called out as I turned to walk away.

I couldn't help but grin. "You in the mood to play hooky?"

Cam didn't smile back. "I don't want to be here," he said.

When I saw the look on his face, I had to walk back. I kneeled down beside him. "Why not? You used to love school."

He shrugged, tightening the straps of his backpack, which was almost as big as he was. "I'd rather be home with you and Mom. Maybe we can give Dad a call. We should see how he's doing..."

I realized then how little attention I'd been paying him, how little contact we'd had in the weeks since Dad had left. He must have been having a hell of a time with all the lies Julian had told and those nasty stories that had scared him and the other kids half to death.

"We'll call him this afternoon when school's over. Sound good?"

Cam seemed to hesitate, and then he grabbed my hand.

"Are you sure we can't just go home?" He seemed desperate.

I squatted down to look him in the eye. "You're safe, Cam. Nobody can hurt you now."

My brother glanced down the hallway and then back at me. It seemed like he had something to say.

"Cam..." I was about to ask him what this was all about, but then he just gave me a hug and sprinted off.

"See you later," I called out, somewhat confused by the way he was acting. Then I looked at my watch. It was late, so I booked it over to the high school wing.

When I reached my locker, I found Ellie leaning against it. I didn't know what to say. But I didn't have to—she spoke first. "I'm so sorry," she said, and her face told me she meant it.

A part of me was angry at her for butting into my relationship—if it wasn't for her, Taylor wouldn't have broken up with me, and he wouldn't be hurting so bad. But I knew the whole thing was actually my fault. I couldn't blame her for something I'd brought upon myself. In the end, I was the one who had deceived Taylor, I had lied to him, and I was so determined not to hurt him that I'd kept things hidden, and that's why we were in this situation.

"It's OK, Ellie," I told her. "With all the shit I'm dealing with right now, the last thing I need is to lose my best friend over a guy."

I opened my locker, took out my books, and closed it again. Ellie smiled, and I noticed she had tears in her eyes.

"Hey, relax," I said, surprised.

"I just screwed up so bad, Kami…" she said, wiping away a tear. "I don't know what it was. I just… I know you're not like that, and seeing my best friend do that to…"

"The guy you have a crush on?" I asked.

Her eyes opened wide, and she shook her head. "I…"

"Seriously, Ellie, it's fine." Just then I saw Taylor standing by his locker at the end of the hall. I was surprised to notice he wasn't alone. Kate was talking to him. Ellie looked over at them, and she was just as surprised as I was.

"What's she up to?"

"I don't know," I replied. Taylor shook his head and looked at my ex–best friend with a baffled expression. He then walked toward us on his way to his and Ellie's AP Physics class. Despite everything that had happened, despite the night I'd spent with Thiago, I couldn't help but feel a twinge of jealousy when he called out to Ellie as he walked by. "You coming, Webber?" he said in that way that made every girl weak in the knees.

Ellie's eyes lit up before she looked to see my reaction.

"See you guys later," I said.

Had Taylor forgotten he'd asked me to talk at lunchtime?

"Good luck on your exam," he said to me, and suddenly my heart started racing.

"What?" I asked, feeling my mouth dry out.

"Your exam," he responded, looking worried. "Kate said you have a final today, right?"

"Shit!"

"Did you forget?" Ellie asked incredulously.

*Fuck!*

"And I thought you'd spent the night studying," Taylor commented, looking me in the eyes.

Was he being sarcastic? Did he know I'd spent the night with Thiago? Had Thiago told him something?

And why did he look distant again—hardened and moody? Why had he been so nice earlier, wanting to talk, only to turn nasty now?

"Fuck. I'm going to fail. Shit, shit, shit…" I said, trying to forget Taylor, Thiago, my brother, my best friend, everything. I had a fucking final!

"You've still got ten minutes to cram," Ellie said, trying but failing to encourage me.

"Bye," I said, running toward class, thinking I could at least look back over the notes. I sat at my desk and read them over, trying to be strategic, telling myself all those letters and numbers were the most important thing in my life. *Memorize, memorize*, I commanded my brain urgently.

What I wouldn't give now to go back to that moment, when my only worries were those of a typical teenager: exams, fights with friends, new love and ex-boyfriends, divorced parents…

It's amazing how we inflate our problems until we let them take over everything in our lives. People always tell us to zoom out and think of all the people who don't even have enough to eat, and those people are right, dammit. TV and newspapers tell us about all the people with real problems. We hear about them every day. And yet we're incapable of realizing how lucky we really are.

We don't get it until we're the ones faced with tragedy, until we're robbed of absolutely everything and reality smacks us in the face—the cold, hard reality that we are nothing but a grain of sand. If we make it through the dangers and misfortunes around us, it's because we're lucky, that's all. If you honestly look at your weaknesses and shortcomings, you realize there's no reason why you should still be alive with all the dangers and threats that surround you.

I'd give anything to go back and do things differently.

But what's the point of looking back when life pushes you forward into the unknown?

# CHAPTER TWELVE

## Kami

No one could have imagined this would happen. Looking back, maybe I could have seen the signs or pinpointed the clues I had somehow managed to convince myself weren't there. I hadn't wanted to see them. Was it fear?

All I know is I did feel something strange that morning when I walked into school. Don't ask me what it was, exactly; it was just something in the air. Call it intuition, a premonition, whatever, but when it happened my mind became awash in relief—not real relief, of course not, but I did feel like a weight had been lifted, as if the pressure I'd been feeling finally had somewhere to go. For weeks, I'd had the strange feeling that something was about to happen, and now I knew why. My brain had kept telling me to be on alert, that something was brewing in those hallways full of teenagers, those classrooms where everyone was pushing themselves to reach the goals society had imposed on us ever since we'd been old enough to talk: *study, pass your exams, get into a good college, get a scholarship, study some more, become crippled with debt, study, work, pay off your loans, work some more, buy a house or an apartment or rent forever, find someone to love you and put up with you, have kids, work, save up so they can go to college, keep working, and so on.*

From now until infinity.

A loud boom made the whole class jump in their seats.

I looked up from my final exam, along with all my classmates, and a shiver ran down my spine. It sounded like gunfire.

Then a second shot followed.

Then a third.

There was a silence that lasted for centuries. Then we heard the screams.

Mr. Dibet stood slowly. I had the urge to do the same. Stand up and run, except not a single muscle in my body reacted, and my classmates were paralyzed, too.

"Someone call 9-1-1," our teacher said, walking toward the door. No one moved.

"What are you waiting for?" he insisted, and finally there was a slight commotion.

In a quivering voice, I responded, "Sir, none of us have our phones."

Mr. Dibet stared at me in pure horror. Then the gun went off again, much closer this time, and I screamed.

"Everyone under your desks! Now!" the teacher ordered us.

We knew the drill, and no one spoke a word, though I could soon hear people whimpering. What were we supposed to do next? Shit, we'd been practicing the protocol for what to do in case of an active shooter ever since we were little, but were we prepared? The fact that it was really happening only reflected just how fucked up the world had become.

Run, hide, fight—that was the protocol, right? Or was it hide first? I looked left and saw Kate, horrified, trembling, hugging herself.

I wished I could say something to her, move to her and wrap my arms around her, feel the warmth of someone who had been my friend since we were kids. It was true we weren't talking anymore, but whatever had happened between us recently didn't matter at that moment.

I heard her whisper something, but her words didn't make any sense to me.

"This is my fault," she said. "My fault."

I squeezed my eyes shut when the next shot rang out. I covered my ears and started praying in silence.

Thiago.

Taylor.

Cameron. Oh my God, Cameron.

That was how the nightmare began.

———

The fire alarm rang through the halls, and I could barely hear the sound of the gunshots. Meanwhile, a voice came over the PA with instructions: "*All students outside immediately!*"

Through all the chaos and noise—how many times had

the shooter fired?—I asked myself how many people might have died already, and how could this possibly be real? Mr. Dibet ordered us all to our feet and said, "We'll walk out single file as quickly as possible. The nearest exit is just a few feet away. The police will be here soon. Let's go!"

We all lined up at the door. When we opened it, what we saw outside was utter chaos.

People were running up and down the halls in terror, pushing past each other to reach the closest exit. And the same thing happened with my fellow students. As soon as the door opened, everyone started to run. Students behind me shoved me to the ground.

"Kami!" Kate yelled just as someone's foot came down on my cheek. I closed my eyes, stunned by the intense pain.

Nobody cared that I was lying there, their feet landing all around me and stomping on the other people who had tripped or been knocked down, the feeling of panic too overwhelming for them to care. I was terrified I'd be trampled to death, but then I felt someone grab my sweater and pull me up. It was Kate.

"Are you OK?" she asked.

My cheek was on fire, but I nodded, and as I looked around, the terror overtook me again. I grabbed Kate's hand, pulled her after me, and shouted, "Come on! We've got to get out of here!" The shots were getting closer, my brain felt like it was short-circuiting, and I was hyperventilating.

Kate screamed, "No! You don't understand, Kami." Jerking me in the opposite direction, she added, "It's my brother, OK? I know it." Again, I was struggling for air, and I felt weak and unable to move. "It's Julian!" she continued. "Julian is the one doing all this."

I shook my head.

No. It couldn't be.

"He put locks on all the doors…"

I heard a boom and an echo, shouts reached our ears, and instinctively, we both crouched down.

I saw blood at the end of the hallway. That was all I needed to react. I grabbed Kate's hand and we ran away from the doors.

My God. This was Julian. Julian was the one responsible for this.

We rushed upstairs, where the science laboratories were, and then I froze when I saw blood pooling in the hallways next to two lifeless bodies on the floor.

"Oh my God," Kate kept saying over and over.

"Don't look," I ordered her. My mind was in a state of panic, as if incapable of registering what had happened only minutes before.

Dozens of thoughts were racing through my head, all of them unsettling, and I couldn't figure out what mattered most. I needed a place where I could stop and think. I pushed open a door to my right and pulled Kate behind me into a classroom that was practically empty except for Ms. Davies. She was lying on the floor, lifeless, her eyes fixed on nothing. Her blouse was soaked with blood, and there was a wound on her head. A dark puddle had spread beneath her, reaching almost to the door. I looked down and realized I'd stepped in it.

"Let's get out of here!" Kate roared. Just then, the fire alarm turned off. There on the second floor, we could hardly hear the shouting, but the whistling of bullets continued.

"Shh," I said, pulling her to me and crossing the room to hide in a cabinet in the back.

"Kami…"

"We're going to hide in there, OK?" I said as I carefully started removing the books and papers stored there to make room for us, as if on autopilot. It was hard to concentrate, but I did my best to make us some space without making a sound. It reassured me to hear that the gunshots were still coming from downstairs.

"Come on!" I whispered, and we got inside, closing the door and crouching down in that tiny space where the two of us could barely squeeze in.

Kate looked like a stranger. I'd never seen fear like that on her face, and I imagined she was thinking the same thing about me.

"Kami," she whispered, controlling the tone of her voice, wrapping her arms around herself, "Julian's not alone."

"What do you mean?" I asked.

It took her a second to respond. "It's not just him. There are others."

That couldn't be. Struggling to keep my voice down, I asked, "What do you mean others? How many? How many, Kate?"

"Two more. They don't go here. They met through his website."

*His website*. The same one Thiago told me about, the one that was full of racist and homophobic content... "How can this be happening?" I asked myself.

"Julian's a psychopath, Kami. And he's obsessed with you."

"Don't say that, please, Kate. Don't try and convince me he's doing this because of me!" It was pointless, because deep down I knew it was true. That didn't mean it was my fault. Julian's obsession with me had turned ugly, and when that group of kids had beaten him up at school a few weeks ago, that had been the last straw.

"He won't stop," Kate declared. "He's coming for you, Kami. He's crazy. You can't imagine the things he's done, the things he's done to me."

Now I was starting to understand why Kate had been acting the way she had. And for once, she was being sincere. She went on: "I tried to stay away from him. I tried to get him to leave me alone. I even talked to my parents. But he can be so weirdly charming when he wants to. And they didn't believe me."

"It's OK, Kate. It doesn't matter anymore."

I tried to calm her down, but she shouted back at me, "You don't understand, Kami!" I couldn't believe she was having an outburst now, when we were in so much danger. I needed her to control herself. If there were two others, one of them could be roving the upstairs halls, and anyone near the biology classroom could have heard her.

No, dammit. I didn't want to die. Not so young.

"Kate, please, be quiet," I begged her.

"He'll know we're here, Kami," she fretted, and in her eyes, I could see it was true. Every word she uttered was sincere and full of terror.

"No," I said. Our hiding place was secure. The school was huge; they couldn't find us, not that fast, and they'd already been in here. If we just stayed quiet, if we just—

"I sent him a text. He knows you're with me," she confessed, taking her phone out of her back pocket.

"What the— You're not supposed to even have your phone on you, Kate! What have you done?"

"It's not my fault! He said he'd kill me if I didn't do it!"

I saw she was about to contact him again, and I grabbed her wrist and squeezed it until she couldn't type another letter. "Are you kidding?" I hissed. "What is wrong with you?"

"He promised me he wouldn't hurt me, Kami. He promised me that if I…"

"Kate, he's lying! Can't you see that? He doesn't care about any of these people!"

"I'm sorry, but I have to try, Kami!"

I didn't give her time to think it over. Instead, I kicked open the cabinet door and ran out. She shouted my name, but I didn't bother looking back. When I reached the stairs at the end of the hall, my mind registered the dead faces on the bodies lying there, even as I tried to look away; those poor people who had just started a normal day at school had now been shot dead. I couldn't help but think how they had tried to escape, just as I was trying to escape now.

I hid under the stairs. I needed to think. I needed to get a grip on my nerves. Clutching my head in my hands, I thought of my brother. Fuck. I needed to find him. I remembered how he'd said he wanted to go home. Had he known something? Had that piece of shit Julian been threatening him again? Had he gotten to him without any of us knowing?

I imagined Cameron hiding, alone and afraid, with no idea where to go. I imagined getting to him too late, having to admit to my parents that I hadn't been able to save him.

I opened my eyes and promised myself I wouldn't let anything bad happen to him.

Where was Taylor? Where was Thiago?

I remembered seeing Kate talking to Taylor. What had she said to him? Was she concocting something fucked-up for him, too? Had Julian given her orders to help find him and kill him the way he wanted to kill me?

Never in my life had I missed my phone the way I did then. Had Julian known we wouldn't be able to use them?

Of course he had. Kate was his spy. She had told him everything that was happening at school. And he had known exactly how to take advantage of what he'd learned.

I didn't know where to go or what to do.

The screaming, the gunshots, they were driving me crazy.

And then I saw them.

One guy. Two. They were armed, and the redheaded one was holding up his pistol to show the other one, a fatter guy with brown hair, who asked if he could try it.

They started to complain there was no one around to shoot at, and I held my breath.

I was petrified, my hands and legs trembling... My heart beat so loudly I was worried the two murderers could hear it. Could this really be happening?

*Don't let me die, Lord. Please don't let me die. And protect my brother and my friends, and Taylor and Thiago, please Lord, don't let them be harmed.*

Where was God when things like this happened? Where was he when we needed him most?

"Where do you think she is?" the brown-haired guy asked.

"I don't know. But I'm sure ready to see what he does with her," the redhead responded.

"I just hope he shares with us." When I heard that, I knew they were talking about me.

I had to get out of there. Now.

# CHAPTER THIRTEEN

## Taylor

AP Physics. A.k.a., a piece of cake. For me, at least. Our exam was next week, and Ms. Dowley kept going over the same problems. I had the material down, and I thought I might lose my mind as she kept repeating herself. How could the rest of the class not get it?

I wasn't paying attention. I didn't need to. I was in the back of the class, with Ellie next to me, and we were writing notes in my notebook. From where we sat, we weren't too worried about the teacher catching us.

Ms. Dowley had stopped chewing me out for not paying attention anyway. At the beginning of the year, she would constantly call me out, and she even gave me detention, but once she saw how good my grades were, she decided to leave me in peace.

I wondered if Ellie got good grades, or if she should be paying attention instead of passing me notes. But I didn't really care. She was making class more fun. *How's your day, Webber?* I wrote and slid the pad back to her.

The day before had sucked. I'd found out my girlfriend

was in love with my brother, and I'd seen that weirdo who was obsessed with her out in the school parking lot. But I had found out Ellie liked me, and that had made me feel good.

I'm not going to lie and say I had my eye on her before. Even now, it wasn't like I was trying to hook up, but she was cool, and she thought I was cool, and even if she was my ex-girlfriend's best friend, I had to admit she was one of the few people who had been straight with me at this school.

*It's 8:20 in the morning. There's your answer*, she replied, eliciting a laugh. I looked up at her. Sitting together had been my idea. Maybe it was wrong, but her company was helping me get over the pain I was trying so hard to hide from the people closest to me.

I was still upset about my fight with my brother, but I wouldn't take back what I said. I wanted him to stay away from me and from Kami. Acting like we could trust each other, like everything was cool—all that was over, it had been for months already.

*Stop complaining and focus on your wave functions*, I wrote and leaned back.

She shot me a killer glare, then jotted down the theorem we were working on from memory. I pulled the notebook away from her and wrote, *Congratulations, you're smarter than you look.*

*Smarter than you, I bet*, she wrote back.

"Di Bianco and Webber, can you pay attention, please?"

We looked up at Ms. Dowley and nodded in silence. But we kept passing notes back and forth, and the questions turned more personal. I have to admit, that was my fault. I don't know why, but I wanted to know more about her: her life, her hobbies, her interests.

I was surprised to find out there was more to her than what I'd thought. For me, she had been the typical pretty cheerleader. But as she told me more about herself, I started to realize why she had been Kami's best friend for so long. Our notes back and forth, and the laughter they provoked, was the best thing so far about the morning. Not that it was hard to outdo arguing with my brother and being reprimanded by the teacher for ignoring her boring explanations.

As class dragged on, Ellie and I slipped into a little world of our own.

But then we heard it. Close.

Too close.

The first shot made us jump out of our seats, and we all fell silent for a second that stretched on like an eternity.

Then the screams came.

And then a lot more shots.

They were coming from the classroom next door. We were petrified, but the real shock came when the door that connected that room with ours seemed to shake and the screams got louder.

I shot up, grabbed Ellie's hand, and pulled her out into the hallway. I could hear other students behind me doing the same a few seconds later.

Just a few seconds. But those seconds were crucial.

It was utter chaos. Nobody knew what to do; none of the stuff we'd learned in protocols as kids did any help. I looked over and saw who was behind this nightmare: a tall guy with a muscular build and an AK-47. He had dark hair in a buzz cut and matching dark eyes. Julian.

As soon as I saw him, I knew this would be the end.

For a lot of people. But almost certainly the end for her.

We ran downstairs in a crowd of students desperate to flee from the slaughter.

All I could see in my mind was the exit. If we made it there, we'd be safe. But that thought wasn't comforting. Because Kami and my brother weren't there, and if they were stuck inside, they'd need help.

What I saw as I reached the hallway on the lower floor was something I don't think I'll ever forget.

The floor was covered in blood and there were bodies, but I couldn't make out their faces. The scariest part was when I noticed two more guys with guns walking the other way down the hall.

I heard Ellie say, "Oh my God" from behind me.

I turned back and pulled her along with me.

Just Julian there was horrible enough. Now there were two others. And who knew if there were more?

How could this be happening?

When had Julian turned into such a monster?

A thought occurred to me, slowly, and with it an intense urge to vomit and a feeling of guilt, of responsibility. I don't know how to explain it, but all I could see in my head was the last time Julian had come to school. The way we'd beaten him up. The way I was happy to jump in.

I know it's not the same thing. I know there was nothing that could compare to the horror being unleashed now, or all the fucked-up things he'd been doing ever since he got to town: his lies, his blackmail, the way he'd frightened poor little Cam, the way he'd abused Kami.

Maybe he was sick. Maybe he was hurting. But nothing in the world could justify this.

"Where are we going?!" Ellie asked, but there was no time to answer. All I could think of was finding the closest exit. I prayed to God we wouldn't run into some other psycho, and I was reassured to hear the gunshots fading away as we ran farther and farther from the main door. The thing was, we'd run away from the only exit. At the back of the building, a group of students had gathered. They seemed desperate, not knowing where to turn.

"We're trapped!"

"We're going to die!"

I scanned the crowd, but Kami and my brother were nowhere to be found.

"Shit!" I yelled. Everyone looked at me, and several people shouted, "Where should we go, Taylor?"

They wanted me to help them. They were begging me. I didn't know who half of them were, but for some reason, they'd decided I could save them. I couldn't take responsibility for all of them. I already had Ellie on my hands. And the more of us there were, the fewer chances we had to make it out alive.

"I don't know," I said. "I…"

"Please," they shouted, "let us go with you…"

Ellie whispered to me, "Come on, Taylor, you can't abandon them."

*Think, Taylor, think, goddammit!*

"To the library," I said. "We're going to the library."

The fire alarms stopped, and so did the gunshots, and an eerie silence ensued. There was whimpering, sobs, shouts. But someone was hunting us, and we needed to keep cool. I silenced the people around me, cursing as I counted them. One, two, three, four... Seven in total. Ellie and me—that made nine. Where the hell was I going to hide nine people?

We made it to the library, and to my surprise, there was no one in there. "Hurry, find whatever you can to block the door," I told them, and we all got to work.

"Will this work?" a younger kid—maybe fourteen—asked, handing me a broomstick.

"Sure," I said, sticking it through the handles on the door. "But it's not enough. Hey, you!" I called to a senior whose name I didn't remember but who was in good shape. "Help me push this bookshelf over."

Everyone else pitched in, and after we got the shelf blocking the door, we pushed a desk behind it, just in case.

"That'll stop them, right?" a dark-skinned girl asked, her voice small. She barely came up to my chest and looked like she was trying hard not to cry.

"Yeah," I lied to reassure her, "it'll definitely stop them." Then, I told everyone to get down so nobody would see them through the windows.

Then I ran to the phone. I remembered how angry I used to get when kids were trying to study and the librarian seemed oblivious, talking loudly with her boyfriend on the landline. But now, that phone was a lifeline. We had to let the outside world know what was going on. Immediately.

Remembering bitterly how our idiot of a principal had forbidden us from bringing our cell phones to class, I dialed 911. The line was busy.

"Shit!"

"What is it?" Ellie asked.

"I can't get through—maybe the lines are jammed."

"That's good, right? It means lots of people are calling, and the police are probably on their way."

I wanted to think so. I wanted to think they'd be here any time.

I walked over to the window and looked out. I could hear sirens and see flashing lights. Police cars were screeching to a halt in the parking lot out front.

I hated to think what was to come. The survivors, if there were any, emotionally shattered, covered in blankets, gathering in front of the school the way I'd seen on TV. And then they'd have to take out the dead. It didn't matter how many—even one death was one too many.

How many lives would be ruined? How many parents would suffer forever, knowing their children had been stolen from them?

I remembered my mother and father, how destroyed they'd been when my sister died. It all played in my mind like a film. And the only thing I could think of was how I would never wish such a thing on anybody. I couldn't let my mother suffer that way. Not again. I had to find Thiago. I had to get these people out of there. I had to save them.

I don't know why, but it felt like a duty suddenly. I had this feeling that my purpose, the reason I had been put there that day, was to save these kids from this hell. It was my obligation, and I accepted it.

And that meant I needed the police to know where we were so they could rescue us. But how? The library's windows were in the back of the building, and the police had parked out front.

The lights went out.

And that's when I knew I'd made a huge mistake.

It was as if I could feel our collective energy vanish in a heartbeat.

"What happened?" a chubby younger kid asked.

Ellie looked at the ceiling. "They've cut the power."

I looked over at the librarian's desk. Her phone was cordless. That meant it wouldn't work. I'd made a terrible mistake; I'd waited too long. I picked it up just in case, and all I heard was dead air. Our one way of getting in touch with the outside world was gone. Julian... Had he known? Had this been part of his plan? Had he somehow cut the lines to the phones in the teachers' lounge, the cafeteria, the office?

I'd had my opportunity to call someone and get out the message that we were locked in the library. I could have called anyone. Anyone could have alerted the cops: my mother, one of my friends from DC.

"SHIT!" I screamed, slamming the phone down and raising my hands in frustration.

And then we all heard a sound.

Holding our breath, we looked at each other.

Did somebody know we were in here?

# CHAPTER FOURTEEN

## Thiago

THE SECOND I HEARD THE SHOTS, ONLY ONE PERSON CAME to mind—her. No one else.

Of course, I remembered my brother next, followed by my students, the teachers, the friends I'd started to make there. But at first, the only thing I could picture was her: her blond hair splayed on the ground, a pool of blood around her, that beautiful, vibrant face suddenly lifeless. That same cold aura my sister's body had when her life was stolen from her after a series of reckless errors.

I knew I would move heaven and earth to find her. I needed her. I needed her alive. I needed that horrible fear to vanish from my mind or I'd never breathe easy again.

I was aching inside, tortured at the realization that the last time we'd seen each other, I'd treated her so coldly. Especially after the night we had shared. I'd done it to keep the peace with my brother, and it was the hardest choice I could ever have imagined. My back was against the wall: it was my family or the girl I loved. Our future together had barely just begun the night before.

As the older brother, I'd had to make choices starting young that I'd never have made if circumstances had been different. And when I saw the pain and disappointment in Taylor's eyes, I knew this wasn't just a typical spat. There was hatred there, resentment, and I couldn't let that fester. I wasn't going to pull my family even further apart, not after everything we had suffered.

Still: The mind is one thing, and the heart is another.

There were four of us in the teachers' lounge when the shooting started: me, Maggie, another teacher from the elementary school, and a high school teacher who'd just come in to say he was heading out—his son had gotten sick at daycare.

The elementary kids were about to arrive—they started an hour later than the older kids. I realized later the only good thing about the whole crazy situation was that the assholes responsible for this bloodbath didn't get a chance to murder any elementary kids.

"Did you hear that?" Maggie asked.

Both of us jumped. I knew that sound. And even though Maggie was my ex, I still felt the urge to protect her. I edged toward the door and heard it again. It sounded like gunshots.

"Call 9-1-1," I told Maggie. But she was too scared to move. Her eyes were empty, the color had drained from her face. Grabbing the phone myself, I shouted to the other three: "Get to the exit. Now! I'll catch up."

As they walked out cautiously, and I heard my heart pounding in my ears, I prayed for someone to pick up. Soon I heard the words *"Nine-one-one, what's your emergency?"*

"There's an active shooting at Carsville High."

"Tell me your name, sir."

"This is Thiago Di Bianco, I'm a coach here. We're in the east wing, where the elementary school is, but the shooting is coming from the high school side. Make sure none of the younger kids try to come inside." I looked at my watch and saw it was quarter to nine. Had any of them arrived yet?

"Sir, the patrol cars are on their way. Are you wounded?"

"No, but—"

That's when I heard it—the screaming. It sounded like the other teachers, my friends—and Maggie.

"Sir?"

I dropped the phone and quickly scanned the room.

On one end of the teachers' lounge was a door that led to the younger children's classrooms, a hallway with bathrooms where the children's arts and crafts projects were displayed. No sooner had I slipped out of the lounge when I heard a voice that made me freeze. Before I could think straight, I hid behind a door, struck with the fear that I might die at the hands of a lunatic.

"Come on! I know you're here!"

It was a voice I didn't recognize. I had to get out of there. If they came through I'd be discovered and killed. I was terrified, but my fear of death vanished when I saw a little pair of blue eyes looking back at me.

"Thiago?"

I didn't hesitate.

I didn't care if I got shot in the back. I didn't care what happened.

They weren't getting him.

Never in my life had I run that way. As I reached Cameron Hamilton, the door to the teachers' lounge opened, making me an easy target.

I heard the shot at the same time as I threw myself across the hallway. It whistled past my left ear and struck a window at the far end of a classroom. I closed the door as fast as I could, dragging a desk in front to block it off. Then I picked Cameron up and took off toward the main hall.

He barely spoke a word. If he hadn't been hanging on to me so tight, I'd have thought he was wounded or worse.

I had to run past the bodies of people who had been my colleagues, including the woman who had been my friend and lover. They'd been shot, and their bodies were lying contorted in pools of blood.

"Don't look," I told Cameron, squeezing him tight as I reached the vestibule. I ducked down, trying to cover the boy with my body as much as I could. I was so afraid, so full of adrenaline, that I wanted to vomit.

Blood.

Screams.

Fear.

This was hell on earth…and I had no idea what to do.

I let my survival instincts guide me, the way I had in the past, the way we all do in situations like these. Except this time, it was different—this was huge compared to anything

I'd been through before. I thought of the pain I'd felt when I lost my sister, and I told myself if I could make sure even one person didn't have to go through that, it would be worth it, even if I had to risk my life. There were too many lives on the line for me to be afraid now…

In Cameron's eyes, I saw horror mixed with blind trust. I was all he had right now. And there was no way I was going to let him down.

I hadn't managed to save Lucy, but I would save little Cam. There was evil in the world, and he was learning about it today, but I wasn't going to let it take him away.

I ran to the cafeteria. I needed a weapon, I kept telling myself, something I could put in my pocket that wasn't a pencil or pen, something I could reach for if these murderers caught me with my guard down. The sound of shots was becoming more distant, which gave me some momentary relief.

"Where are we going, Thiago?" Cameron asked, so scared I could barely hear him.

"We're going to hide in the cafeteria. Everything will be fine."

The halls were empty—no killers, no bodies, no signs of life or death.

Now that I think about it, I should have done something different. It would have been better to try and hide among the carnage. Because for three armed psychos, those empty rooms and halls were like a blank canvas, a sign of defeat.

The cafeteria was empty, too. I was confused. Where were they?

We walked behind the counter into the kitchens. There was nothing on the stainless-steel counters. This was where Ms. Puck, one of the cooks, usually stood. She was a tall and imposing woman older than my mother who had been nice to me ever since I'd started working there. She always gave me a second piece of chocolate cake when I asked. I was relieved not to find her now, hoping that her shift hadn't started yet.

I put Cameron down and told him to stay by the door while I went in the back where the loading docks stood to receive daily deliveries for the hundreds of students at Carsville. I felt so relieved when I saw the door because it meant a way out of this nightmare. All I wanted was to get Cameron to safety so I could go find Kam and my brother, make sure they were OK, too, and bring them back here to escape.

I pushed and pushed on the door, but it wouldn't move an inch.

"They're locked," I heard a soft voice say.

I turned and found Cameron with his eyes full of tears.

"How do you know?"

Cam looked around, unsure what to say, squeezing a little stuffed dinosaur he'd been carrying the whole time without my noticing. He gazed up at me with a pleading expression, as if he needed me to tell him it wasn't his fault.

"He forced me," he responded as I came closer. "He forced me to help him…"

"Who forced you, Cameron?"

"Momo," he responded with terror in his eyes.

"Momo isn't real."

"He is, too, real! And he forced me! He forced me to lock it…"

I could feel the blood drain from my face.

"Did you see him, Cam?"

"Yeah. And he looked just like he does on the internet."

Dammit. He must have had on a mask. "Why didn't you tell your mother or Kami?"

"Because he said if I told anyone he'd hurt Juana!"

Juana…that damned iguana. Whoever was behind this was a sick bastard.

"It's OK," I said, hugging him tight and trying to calm him down. "It's OK, little guy… But I need you to listen to me very, very closely. If you and Momo are both in here, then there must be one door that's still open. Which doors did you lock?"

Cameron thought for a few seconds and said, "Just two. The gym and the cafeteria…"

In my mind, I drew a map of the school, trying to figure out which door was likeliest to be open. The auditorium, maybe? That was nowhere near the kitchen. I tried to ignore the horror, my hatred for Julian—because it was Julian. Who else could it be? I felt guilty. I should have taken him more seriously, I should have done more to convince the police that he wasn't just some teenage runaway… Maybe I should have killed him when I had the chance.

But none of that mattered now. I needed to focus.

Cameron and I looked up when we heard the sound

of helicopters overhead. And then I saw it: the skylight. It was big enough to fit through. We just needed to be careful climbing up, and it would lead us to the roof.

"Cam, over here!" I said, standing directly under it.

I just needed a ladder and something to break it with. But where in the hell would I get a hammer?

Cam must have known what I was thinking, because he said, "It's too high."

"Fuck!"

I looked all around. The windows were reinforced glass, they'd be almost impossible to shatter, and they only opened a few inches. Unless the police showed up with battering rams, that option was out. As I looked back at Cam, I heard a terrifying voice come over the PA.

*"Attention, students. Despite what you might think, my intention isn't to kill you. Not all of you, anyway. You'll be allowed to leave, one by one, if you help me fulfill today's mission, a mission I've been planning for months, a mission to rid you of the scum who walk among you."*

I shivered with recognition. It was distorted, but I'd recognize it anywhere. I couldn't help clenching my fists. When I saw the fear on Cam's face, I realized that this was the same voice, speaking through some kind of masking device, that had threatened him and forced him to do things he'd never have done otherwise.

"Relax, buddy," I told him, and we looked up again, listening to the words of the madman.

*"I'll make it very easy on you. Just bring me the people on the list I'm about to read out, and after that, you can go.*

*Let me repeat: If you bring me these losers, you can leave, one by one, without a scratch on you."*

He then began to name off not random students, but basketball players, cheerleaders... I shuddered as I heard the guys from my team called out, their girlfriends, the popular kids, the elite...

*"Danny Walker, Harry Lionel, Ellie Webber, Aaron Martin, Victoria Tribecky, Amanda Church, Victor Di Viani, Marissa Digeronimo, Chloe Harrison..."*

And the names went on, until he had reached twenty students. He paused, and I tensed up as he spoke again: *"And now, for the final three. The stars of the show. You all know them, you've all wanted to be them, we've all fallen at their feet. How can you resist the two brothers who look like they stepped out of a fricking Hollywood film? You know who I mean, right, girls? The ones you all slobber over like bitches in heat. I'm talking about the Di Bianco brothers. And finally, the person who ruined my life as soon as I laid eyes on her..."*

Cam was staring at me with terror in his eyes. And I, too, was shaking as I guessed which name would come next.

*"She's the girl you all love and hate, the girl who doesn't have to do anything to light up the room...the girl who played with my heart, who trapped me with her eyes and her smile, and who threw me out like a broken toy..."*

"You son of a bitch," I murmured under my breath.

*"I heard what you said about me, Kamila: 'You guys see him as some kind of danger, but for me, he's just a*

*pathetic loser who had to lie to me and lie to himself to make friends. He's a creep, a liar. He's a pathetic asshole, and he's going to spend the rest of his life alone.'"*

What the...? Those were the same words Kam had said the day she'd been walking to school, the day Taylor and I had gotten angry with her for not watching her back because Julian was still out there... He'd been listening to her somehow...following her.

*"But who's going to be alone now, Kamila? You. Because I'm going to kill everyone you love right in front of your eyes. And then I'll finish you off. Because you don't deserve to live after what you did to me. If I can't have you, then no one can."*

Cam was holding on to my leg tight, and I was so stunned I couldn't even find the words to calm him down.

*"If you want this to stop, bring me the people on my list... especially Kamila."*

The PA system screeched, echoing all around me, and that was the last thing I heard before the cafeteria door flew open.

# CHAPTER FIFTEEN

## Kami

I WAS SHAKING.

My whole body was trembling, and there was nothing I could do to calm down.

I had seen the bodies of my classmates. I'd seen them murdered in cold blood. My school had become a living hell… And the carnage was my fault.

*But who's going to be alone now, Kamila? You. Because I'm going to kill everyone you love right in front of your eyes. And then I'll finish you off. Because you don't deserve to live after what you did to me. If I can't have you, then no one can.*

*I'm going to kill everyone you love.*

*I'm going to kill everyone you love.*

*I'm going to kill everyone you love.*

I couldn't stop hearing those words over and over in my head, and each time I felt reality closing its grip around my throat. I felt my stomach turn and the overwhelming urge to vomit.

I rested my hands on the floor and tried to breathe.

I was alone.

And there was no one I could ask for help.

Would my classmates hand me over?

Would they do it, knowing that would mean certain death?

Of course they would. Who wouldn't, knowing that this entire nightmare was my fault?

*But it's not YOUR fault!* a voice in my head shouted.

*You were nice to him! You were his friend! He was the one who betrayed your trust! He was the one who invaded your privacy! He was the one who manipulated your little brother to steal your things!*

I took a deep breath and looked down the hall.

The two killers had turned the corner heading toward the cafeteria. Julian had to be in the principal's office to use the PA system, which meant for the moment, I was out of danger...

Was this my chance?

Going to look for my brother would be impossible with those two murderers roving the halls. All I could do was pray that Cameron had gotten away or found somewhere to hide. He had a talent for that—when I played hide-and-seek with him, I could almost never find him—and I prayed he'd found somewhere safe until I could come for him.

I had no idea where to go, but I needed to move: there, under the stairs, I was exposed with nowhere to run to if anyone saw me.

Terrified, walking softly, I headed toward the library.

I tried not to think, tried not to look at the dead bodies along the way, but I couldn't help it; I needed to know if I'd lost any of my friends, to make sure Taylor wasn't lying there, or Thiago, or Ellie…

It felt like miles from the stairs to the library, walking past the classrooms and feeling my heart pounding out of control. I don't know how I did it, how I even managed to move with that fear that had seeped into every fiber of my being, dense and overwhelming. And every ounce of adrenaline in my body was pumping through my veins to keep my feet on the move.

When I arrived at the library, I tried to push the door, but it wouldn't budge.

Hearing muffled voices, I knew there were students inside.

"Let me in, please!" I said as loudly as I could, given the circumstances.

I heard murmurs, bodies moving, and for the first time since this nightmare had begun, I felt a slight sense of relief.

"Kami?!"

"Taylor?!"

"Help me," I heard him say, then I heard something dragging along the floor. The door opened. There he was. We ran toward each other, his arms enclosed me, and I buried my head in his chest. Then he stepped back, pulling me inside, and everyone else blocked the door again.

"Are you OK?" he asked me. "Are you hurt?" He looked me all over, trying to see if I had any marks on me. Noticing the bruise on my right cheek, he asked me what had happened. But I couldn't respond. In pain, in terror, I burst into tears. All the tension that had built up inside me finally broke free. I felt ravaged.

Ravaged, because I still couldn't believe this was happening. Ravaged, because seeing Taylor alive made me realize how much I could have lost...

"Easy... Easy, babe," he said, holding me tight.

All eyes in the library were on us, and I wanted to look around and see who was in there, but I tried not to, because doing so would force me to take stock of how many of us hadn't made it. Besides, two very important people were obviously still missing.

Taylor walked me to the far corner of the library where we could be alone and looked me in the eyes.

"Are you all right?" he asked, looking at my bruise. I could feel it swelling by the second.

"I fell on the ground and someone kicked me... Taylor... Taylor, what's happening? How can this be real?"

"We've got to get you out of here. We've got to get everyone out of here," he said, pulling me in close again. He was so scared. "I can't... I can't believe you're here," he said. "I thought... I thought..."

I looked him in the eye to let him know the same thought had crossed my mind.

"Taylor, Kate knows everything... She knew it was going to happen, and she tried to tell Julian where I was so he could come for me..."

A flash of insight lit Taylor's eyes. "This morning..." he said, "Kate told me she had something important she needed to tell me and that she'd wait for me by the front door during second period..."

"Julian wanted her to hand us over to him. If she did, he said he'd let her live. He's crazy, Taylor. He's crazy, and he'll kill us all."

As I was saying this, someone walked up behind me. I turned around and saw it was Ellie. I cried out her name, relieved, as close to happy as a person could be given these hideous circumstances. As we embraced, I said, "I can't believe you're here."

She was crying as she informed me, "Kami... I saw Chloe... She was lying on the ground... There was blood all around her."

I felt a part of my heart being torn away.

Chloe and I had been friends since we were kids. We'd never been as close as Kate or Ellie and I had, but there had always been something special between us. She was the crazy girl, the one always tempting us to get in trouble...

As Ellie and I held each other, all I could do was pray to God to protect us, and to please bring this living nightmare to an end. Ellie looked over my shoulder and told me, "I don't know how to tell you, but people are saying..." Her voice was filled with dread.

She couldn't bring herself to finish the phrase. Taylor had a serious look on his face as he motioned for us to follow him back to the main room in the library. There weren't many people there: I recognized one girl from my math class and some others I had passed in the hallways. They were all terrified, especially the middle schoolers. One tall kid stepped forward, frowning at us, but Taylor stopped him with an icy glare, asking, "What the hell is going on?"

The kid wasn't daunted. Looking back at his friends, he took another step and said, "You heard the guy, right? You three are on the list."

Taylor spread his arms to protect us. "You'd better not be insinuating what I think." I'd never heard him sound more serious in my life. Two other kids stepped forward, flanking the tall one.

"Why should we have to pay for whatever you guys did?" the one on the right said. He was a little bigger than the other two.

"There are little kids here! Are you guys really selfish enough to risk our lives and theirs over something you did?" the one on the left said as everyone else watched the scene, entranced.

I had been scared of this when I'd heard Julian's distorted voice over the loudspeaker. And now it was happening before my very eyes.

Fearless, Taylor stared the three of them down and said, "What are you suggesting? You want to drag us out of here and watch them kill us?"

As they faced off, I thought of all the things that might happen. Taylor was strong, but could he really take all three of these guys fighting for their lives? And what if the others jumped in? What would Ellie and I do? Thousands of scenarios shot through my mind, and all of them ended badly.

One of the guys told Taylor, "Sorry, dude. But I don't feel like dying. This has to stop, and there's only one way."

Just then, we heard helicopters whirring overhead again, and as we looked up, a voice came over a megaphone. It came as a great relief: "*This is the Carsville chief of police. Whoever the shooters are, drop your weapons and come out with your hands up. I repeat, drop your weapons and come out with your hands up.*"

We all held our breath, listening to the choppers.

If only we could reach the roof...

"Do they honestly think these bastards are just going to walk out with their hands in the air?" Ellie asked in shock.

"They won't give up until they've done what they came here to do," the most muscular of the three guys, the one who had just told Taylor he wanted to hand us over, shouted.

"Listen, shithead," Taylor said—I cringed because provoking those guys when we were at a clear disadvantage was probably the worst strategy—"if you threaten me again, I swear to God those will be the last words you ever say."

This was getting out of hand. The three guys were trying to surround him. We had to get out of there. We needed to leave the library before a fight broke out, or before the shouting got loud enough to alert the killers to our location. Ellie gripped my hand.

Out of nowhere, a girl yelled, "Stop it! Can't you hear what you're saying? What proof is there that they're actually going to let us go if we turn them in? Do you think you can trust a bunch of murderers? The best thing we can do is wait here and let the police do their jobs!"

The room fell silent as everyone thought about what to do.

"It'll be too late by the time the police come inside," the tallest of the three boys said.

"You don't know that! You're not a cop!" the girl responded. "You don't know anything. An hour ago, I heard you saying how lucky we were to follow Taylor in here, that we'd found a good hideout. You were grateful to be alive, and now you want to hand him and his friends over and just let them die?!"

"Shut up!"

"Stop it!" Taylor shouted, and before we knew it, they were at each other's throats. Taylor didn't throw the first punch, but he dodged it in time to hit that asshole square on the cheek. Then the tall guy jumped in, and suddenly it was three against one, with the rest of us watching helplessly.

And then things got even worse, because we heard gunshots.

We stopped and held our breath, afraid of what would come next.

We all ran away from the door and hid as best we could. I didn't know who I was more scared of: Julian and his friends with the guns, or my classmates, who followed us with their eyes, ready to sacrifice us.

How could they?

Taylor grabbed Ellie and me by the wrists and dragged us past row after row of shelves, past the study rooms, past the computers, past the newly installed audiovisual area.

When we reached the far wall, we got down on our hands and knees.

"We can't stay here," Taylor said, looking at the two of us very sternly.

"We can't leave, though; what if the killers see us?" Ellie replied in terror.

"Trust me, the other kids won't hesitate to hand us over. They're scared; there's nothing they won't do if they think it'll help them make it out alive," Taylor replied.

I couldn't believe what people were capable of when they felt overrun by fear. Our friends, our classmates, the people we'd shared notes with and gone to games with, were now ready to throw us to the dogs.

"How, then?" I asked. "Where are we going to go?"

Taylor thought a moment, then said the same thing I'd been thinking: "We need to make it to the roof. Once we're there, the helicopters can pick us up. There are skylights in several rooms. That might even be where the cops are thinking of coming in."

"How are we going to get to the roof, though?" I asked.

The three of us looked at each other and shook our heads. Taylor repeated that we had to escape the library first and find a better hiding place.

"Taylor," I told him, "I can't leave without my brother. I have to find him… I don't know if he made it out on his own, if he's hiding somewhere, or if he's…"

I burst into sobs; I couldn't finish the phrase, and Taylor tried to console me: "Thiago knows Cam's here, and he usually hangs out in the teachers' lounge at the elementary school in the mornings. He wouldn't abandon your brother. I promise you that. Cameron's safe."

That hadn't occurred to me, but it was true. Thiago was almost always in the other wing. Had he found my brother? Had he known where Cam would be? Had the killers stayed away from the elementary school?

Ellie pulled me out of these thoughts, asking, "What's the plan, then?"

Taylor peeked around the corner of a shelf. "There's no reasoning with them. And there's no way out except the same door we came in through."

"But what if the killers are just waiting for us outside?" I asked.

I could see the fear in his eyes, and his mind working at top speed, asking himself how we could escape not just our classmates, but the killers, too. He concluded, "Look, they'll come for us sooner or later. It's just a matter of time until they reach the library. When they do, that's our one chance. I know it sounds terrifying, but we're going to have to push past the other kids and run like hell."

# CHAPTER SIXTEEN

## *Thiago*

I pulled Cameron behind the kitchen door and motioned for him to stay silent as I looked around desperately for a better place to hide.

"I told you there was no one in here," I heard a voice say. It was the same guy who had been chasing Cameron and me before.

"I heard something," someone else said.

How many of them were there?

"We should go to the library. I'll bet there's all kinds of people in there."

"Jules told us to look everywhere. And that's what I'm going to do."

I peeked through the crack in the door and saw them clearly. One was chunky, the other had red hair, and they had rifles slung over their shoulders and pistols in their hands. I looked at the terrorized kid next to me and I knew I had to get him out of here, but how? Without a ladder, there was no way of making it to the roof, and the only one I could think of was in the utility room, all the way on the other side of the school. How the hell would I get there and back without anyone seeing me?

*You need a distraction*, a voice in my head told me. *A distraction that won't endanger the seven-year-old boy next to you.*

It was then that I heard one of them say: "Go look in the kitchen."

I had to think fast. Faster than I'd ever thought in my entire life.

I took Cameron's hand and walked him into dry storage. All around us were canned foods, bottles of sauce, bags of potatoes, and industrial-sized packs of seasoning.

*Think. Think.*

I looked up. Everything was stacked on industrial-strength steel shelves. They were bolted to the wall and would hold our weight, but we wouldn't be able to stay there in silence for long.

"Cam, buddy, climb up there," I told him as I looked around for something to cover us. When my eyes landed on a pile of towels and aprons, I knew it was our only hope. I grabbed as many as I could, hoisted myself up on the shelf, and spread them over the top of us. It wasn't much, but it was our only hope. Realizing this, I pressed my back tight into Cameron. If they did find us, maybe they wouldn't see him behind me, and at least one of us would live. I whispered, "Listen, buddy. We're going to be OK. But I need you to be absolutely quiet until I tell you it's all right to talk again. Don't cough, and try as hard as you can not to make any noise when you breathe."

I couldn't see him, but I felt his little head nodding.

They were in the kitchen now, but it was big, and they were taking their time. I couldn't believe it, but it sounded like they were unwrapping the granola bars meant for the elementary school kids' snacks and eating them. I knew Cam was scared, and I knew he'd soon get antsy, so I reached back very slowly, being sure not to shift any of the fabric on top of us, to pat him on the knee.

I heard a creaking sound. The door opening. We were trapped. For some reason, they started pulling things off the shelf and onto the floor, kicking the flour bins, tossing aside a bag of onions. But then one of them said, "There's nobody here," and the other responded, "Yeah, let's get a move on. You heard Jules read the list out. There's still a bunch of them left."

The horror of discovering they'd already killed some people on the list made my stomach turn. My brother and Kam—were they still alive? Had they been killed in cold blood like so many others?

I waited a few extra minutes, then got down as quickly and quietly as I could. Cameron crawled to the edge of the shelf and held his arms out for me to grab him. I shook my head.

"You need to stay up there, buddy," I told him.

"No! I want to go with you!"

"Cam, you can't. It's dangerous. You saw what these guys are capable of." He started crying, and I continued, "Listen to me. Stay here. I'm going to go find a ladder so we can reach the skylight. You're safe here. They're not coming back, and once I can get us out on the roof, we'll be safe."

At last, he nodded, silent tears still streaming down his face. "Are you scared?" he asked me.

My heart aching, I told him honestly, "Hell yeah, I'm scared, pal. But everything's going to be OK. I'm getting you out of here."

"What about Kami and Taylor?"

"Them, too. We'll all make it to the roof. We'll all be safe."

He nodded, and I smiled at him as best I could. Then I thought of something and said, "Cam, hold on. I'll be right back."

I went to the kitchen, looked around in the drawers, and took out two knives. I walked back into the pantry and found Cameron looking a little calmer. "Here," I said, handing one to him. I was worried about what I was about to tell him—I didn't want to traumatize him further—but this was no time for speeches, so I spit it out: "Use this if you have to. If anyone tries to hurt you, stick it straight in their eye, OK?"

I pointed out the exact place, and the boy nodded, scared and serious.

"I'll be back for you. I promise."

I covered him up again with a couple of aprons and stuffed the other knife I had grabbed in my back pocket.

Now came the hard part.

# CHAPTER SEVENTEEN

## Kami

THEY DIDN'T TAKE LONG. TAYLOR HAD BEEN RIGHT. IT was the same guys I'd seen close to the stairs. I could tell by their voices. And he was right about something else, too: As soon as danger was near, our classmates didn't hesitate to rat us out.

"Open the door!" the two guys yelled, first pushing, then shooting, causing everyone gathered in the library to scream. No one tried to stop them, and as soon as the doors opened, everyone started yelling.

"They're over there!"

"The ones from the list! Kamila Hamilton, Ellie Webber, and Taylor Di Bianco! They're right there!"

How could they do this to us? I grabbed Ellie's hand and looked at Taylor, horrified.

"Run. I'll distract them," he said. We both shook our heads, and I told him, "No."

"I said go!" he ordered us. And before I could refuse again, Taylor had stood up and taken off. I looked at Ellie, unsure what he was up to and with no idea what to do.

That was when I heard one of the guys say, "You take that side, and I'll take this one."

Shit. They were going to split up. Suddenly, Taylor took off running away from the door to the other side of the library. "There he is!" one shouted just as I called out his name, terrified that something would happen to him.

"Come on!" Ellie said, pulling me behind her. "This is our only chance!"

We ran desperately toward the door, our only possibility for escaping the massacre, but then the three guys who had been fighting with Taylor before got in our way. We were dead, I thought. But something I would never have expected happened. The five others who were with us, girls and guys both, jumped on them, catching them by surprise and giving us just enough time to get out. "Run!" a girl yelled after me. Little did she know that would be her death sentence.

I didn't look back. Ellie didn't let me. We sprinted down the hall, running for our lives, in desperate hope of escape. And then the worst happened.

We were at the end of the hall, about to turn the corner, and my legs were just about to give out when a slew of bullets came whizzing past me, so I threw myself on the ground, covering my head. Then I heard a voice behind me shout, *No!* and I waited for the pain, waited to feel what so many other students had already experienced at the hands of those sick bastards, waited to feel the warm blood seep through my clothes as my eyes closed and I lost consciousness. But none of that happened.

Instead, everything turned to slow motion. You see that

in movies, the way a traumatic or near-death experience slows things down and a person can see everything happening all at once, perceiving every single detail, even as so many emotions blend together. In slow motion, I saw my best friend falling. I wanted to go to her, hold her in my arms, and tell her everything would be OK, but I snapped out of it when I heard a familiar voice.

"Kami, run!" Taylor shouted, and everything sped back up to warp speed.

I struggled to get up, but was spurred on by rage and pain, so I ran. When I turned the corner, I saw him.

There he was.

Thiago.

"Kam!"

His voice pronouncing my name, and just finding him alive, all but paralyzed me.

I don't know how I reached him, I don't even know how my legs were still moving, all I know is suddenly he was holding me in his arms, his body wrapped around me, protecting me. Then we were no longer in the hallway, he'd pulled me somewhere small and dark, a dusty broom closet. I was in Thiago's arms... Finally, I was back in his arms.

"Kamila," he said, his hands on my cheeks, his eyes taking me in. I was blinking, almost as though my tears hoped to wash away that image of Ellie on the ground... Then I saw him, I really saw him, the love of my life, the only person with whom I could imagine regaining some semblance of normalcy after all that violence, desperation, blood, and death.

"She got shot," I managed to say after several seconds in silence.

Looking back, I realize I must have been in a state of shock. I remember him whispering tender, sweet nothings in my ear, but I don't remember what he said. At some point I came back to reality and found myself there in that dark, ugly place, that refuge where I felt the full weight of sadness, death, and despair.

Thiago asked me who had been shot. His voice was soft, but his eyes were scared.

"Ellie," I told him. "It was Julian. Julian's the one doing this."

I had seen him when Ellie and I were running. It was him shooting at us, not the others. Julian had emerged from his hiding place and shot my best friend without a second thought.

He could have shot me, too, but he hadn't. He'd said over the PA system that he wanted to wait. That what he wanted was to see me suffer, watching all the people I most loved disappear.

I heard Thiago trying to soothe me, inhaled his familiar scent, felt his warmth, and I emerged from my trance. I opened my eyes, pulled away, stared at him, and said his name: "Thiago?"

"Yeah, babe, it's me." His eyes were watering, full of emotion. "I was so scared, I was so scared you were gone."

"I'm here," I interrupted him, trying to pull myself together, trying to suppress my fear and sorrow, trying not to think of the dead, and instead focusing on the fact that he was with me. The one person I could get through this with—if only, if only I had known what was coming, if only I had known how long I would have to wait for another chance like this one.

"Thiago, we've got to get out of here. They're going to kill us all."

Had Taylor managed to escape? I didn't know. Had one of the guys in the library gotten to him? Had Julian?

"Taylor helped us," I said, hearing a change in Thiago's breathing. "We were in the library, these guys wanted to hand us over, they thought that way they could save themselves. It was horrible. And Taylor told us to run. And then Ellie— I don't know if he made it out. I only looked back once."

"Taylor's alive?" Thiago asked.

"He was. A minute ago he was. Now…"

I fell silent. Not just because Thiago covered my mouth with his massive hand, but because I, too, heard voices outside. Thiago lowered his hand but gestured for me to remain silent.

"I want them alive, you hear me? I want those three alive and kicking," Julian commanded, and I shuddered at the sound of his voice.

I remembered the last time we'd talked before I learned that he was stalking me, before I learned that our friendship, his whole persona, everything, was a lie… He was sick, he was crazy—but what he said next pushed me over the edge.

"We can't find the kid, Jules," one of his goons said.

"Well, he's got to be somewhere. Find him, dammit! He's seven fucking years old. He can't have gone far!"

Thiago held me tight, pushed me against the wall and pressed his hand to my lips so I wouldn't scream. My little brother. My poor little brother. Cameron.

Once they were gone, Thiago held my face in his hands. "Listen," he said, "your brother's fine. He's safe."

"You saw him?" My voice was quivering and I wanted to cry, but the tears didn't come. This moment was too critical; I had to block off all my fears if I wanted to make it out alive. There would be time enough later to break down and cry. For now, I needed to get a grip.

"Yeah," Thiago said. "He's hiding."

"Hiding? Where?" I couldn't believe it. I thought he'd made it out. The poor little kid, he was still inside, and it was a death trap for anyone I loved or cared about. "Take me to see him," I went on. "I need to see him."

I tried to open the door, but Thiago grabbed my hand and said, "Kam, he's safe. I promise you. Now focus. I'm going to get us out of here. We'll go out through the roof. Once we're there, the helicopters will see us and they'll rescue us."

Taylor had said the same thing to Ellie and me. Get to the roof. But how?

I asked him, and he responded, "There's a skylight in the cafeteria. It's big enough to squeeze through. And your brother's there, in the kitchen. He's hiding. They won't see him."

"Take me to him," I said. I needed out, now. I needed

to see with my own eyes that my brother was all right, that he was alive.

"We need a ladder first," he said, pinching the bridge of his nose.

He looked so tired. So tired, and so afraid.

"There's one ladder in the utility room. If we can get there and take it to the cafeteria—"

"We can get out," I finished for him.

"That's right," he confirmed.

Our eyes met. I looked into those beautiful green eyes, eyes that had once made me tremble but now felt soothing because I knew with him, I was safe, I knew he would help me escape this hell. All the emotions inside me surged together. "Thiago," I said. But there were no more words to express what I was feeling. I saw something in his eyes: not just terror, but love, promises that couldn't be spoken now. And that's when it happened.

Our lips met, and it was nothing like any other kiss we'd shared before. This kiss was special because I knew it might be our last. My back was against the wall, his hands sought me out desperately; it was as if he needed to feel every inch of me, treasure the heat of my body, remind himself that I was his.

For that brief moment, there was nothing in the world but the two of us. The horror outside ceased to exist.

His hands touched my face, tracing my every feature. His mouth drank my tears, and we kissed until we ran out of breath. I knew then it was him—my heart belonged to him alone.

"I love you," he said. "Don't ever forget that, OK?"

I blinked to see him more clearly. "Promise we'll make it out alive—promise me when it's over, we'll be together. Promise you'll take me with you wherever you go, that you'll follow me anywhere. Promise there won't be a day where we don't say *I love you*, that we'll never be apart. Promise me that you'll put us first, before everything else, and I promise you I'll do the same. I know life is short. And whatever's left of it, I want to spend it with you."

His eyes told me everything and nothing. Why was he holding back? Why was he hesitating?

His lips parted, and he uttered the magic words. The only words I needed to gather the courage to open that door and face whatever lay out there.

"I promise."

I knew it now: I was strong enough to continue.

He smoothed my hair, tucked a lock of it behind my ear, and kissed the tip of my nose.

"Are you ready?" he asked.

I nodded, and we opened the door and stepped into hell.

# CHAPTER EIGHTEEN

## *Taylor*

EVERYTHING HAPPENED SO QUICKLY. ALL I KNEW WAS THAT I'd had no choice: I'd had to distract those fuckers so Ellie and Kami could escape.

I moved quickly, throwing books and chairs to get the guys' attention, then ran toward the door myself.

I was grateful that some of the other kids had helped the girls get out instead of handing them over the way those three dickheads had wanted. If they hadn't, I'd never have gotten out myself, because I couldn't have just abandoned them.

Once in the hall, my mind took in everything instantly: Ellie and Kami at one end, turning the corner to find a hiding place, and Julian at the other, aiming his pistol in cold blood.

"*NO!*" I shouted, feeling my throat clamp up. I couldn't let them die. I couldn't bear the thought of either of them being gone. I had to save them. Protect them. But I didn't know what more I could do.

When I saw them hit the ground, I thought the worst.

Two shots. One for each of them.

Had they been hit?

I wanted to run over to them, throw myself on top of them, but my survival instinct took over, and I found myself hiding from Julian. Either he hadn't seen me or hadn't cared once he saw his real target in front of him. The girl he blamed for all his problems. The girl he had been obsessed with for months. The girl he'd dreamed of since he first saw her.

It was Kami he really wanted, and I wasn't surprised he hadn't wasted time on me when she was just a few feet away.

His obsession had saved me.

And my subconscious had taken advantage of that, even when my conscious mind had refused to.

I hid.

But I didn't go far.

I ducked into the classroom right across the hall.

Through the window, I could see the kids who had been in the library—they were escaping. I saw Julian chasing Kami. She had gotten up, and I was praying she'd find a place to hide.

Then the two other shooters followed.

Once there was nothing but a deafening silence in the hallway, I hurried out to where Ellie lay, praying to God she wasn't dead. I fell to my knees in a pool of her blood where her chestnut hair framed her face.

"Come on, Webber," I said, my hand to her cheek, "don't do this to me."

She was unconscious, but when she heard my voice, she blinked her eyes open, giving me hope.

"Ellie, please," I said, cradling her in my arms, "you're

going to be fine, I promise." My voice cracked so much that she probably couldn't even understand me. My face was awash in tears.

"T-Taylor…" she stuttered.

"Shhh," I said, rocking her softly. "Don't speak…"

"I like you, T-Taylor…" Blood trickled from her mouth, and more was seeping out of the bullet wounds in her torso.

"I know, I know…" I said with a sharp pain in my chest.

"I w-wish we could have g-gone out," she confessed. Was she smiling at me? Was that really possible?

"I'd have liked that," I responded, trying not to look at her wounds. I looked beyond the blood, at the person she had been, the person she really was. And my mind was flooded with images of her. Ellie smiling. Ellie stopping on the court to say hi on her way to cheerleading. Ellie getting into arguments with everyone in the cafeteria, Ellie pretending to grimace when I walked past her and made some dumb remark.

The way she'd nibble at her nails, the way she seemed able to use literally anything to pull her hair up: a pen, a pencil, a chopstick, a fork…

Her smile was gorgeous; I remembered her shining it on me once in a while when I cracked a joke. Had I been flirting with her without knowing it? Was that why I'd liked getting on her nerves?

"You've always been such a pain in the neck," I said, and she winced in pain, trying to smile at me.

"Y-you always thought you were the sh—the shit," she countered.

I smiled, stroking her hair, and said, "You should have told me you liked me."

"Y-you f-fell for the wrong p-person." She coughed, and I had to raise her torso so she could breathe better.

"Hey, easy... Don't talk, OK?" I said in despair, because her life was slipping through my fingers and there was nothing I could do about it.

"Do me a f-favor?" she said. "H-have a good life."

I nodded, looking into her bright, beautiful eyes.

I knew then I was losing a person that mattered. And it hurt more than I could have imagined.

Following my instincts, knowing I would never have that chance again, I leaned over and gently laid my lips on hers. She squeezed my hand and used all her strength to try and hold me closer. My heart was pounding.

I didn't pull away until I knew she was no longer with me.

————

I didn't know where to go or what to do.

I was desperate, I was sad, I was scared. I imagined finding Kami or my brother splayed out on the ground like Ellie.

I couldn't stop thinking about the last words I'd spoken to Thiago, how little time we'd spent together since the school year started, the damage we had done to each other.

How had we come to this?

I swore to myself that if we lived through this, I'd start looking at life differently. I wouldn't suffer over a girl. I wouldn't allow a single day to pass without letting the people around me know that I loved them.

I'd watch TV with Mom, even if it was just that stupid romantic shit she couldn't get enough of on Netflix. I'd throw my arm around her on the couch and veg out until we fell asleep. I'd plan trips with my brother, shoot hoops with him in our free time, do all the stuff we used to do when we were little. As for Kami... Well, I'd do whatever it took, but if we couldn't be together, I wasn't going to force it. I'd let her go, and if that meant letting my brother have her, then I'd accept it and go on with my life.

I had made a promise to Ellie, and I was going to keep that promise.

I raced through the halls, not knowing what to do, looking for a way out, an open door, anything. Other students stopped me, asked me where to go, what to do, but I ignored them and went on my way.

Every few minutes, I heard shouts—screams. I couldn't imagine there were many people left alive, and worse, no one seemed to be doing anything to save the few of us left, fighting to survive. The cops were still outside; the ambulances were waiting—we were alone.

Why?

Why, dammit?!

Then they found me.

Julian and his cronies.

They beat me to a pulp, of course. Three against one...and the leader of those three hated me and blamed me for all his problems.

Looking back, I wondered what would have happened if Thiago had thought I was dead, if he hadn't heard that message over the PA and knew I was still alive.

I bet everything would have been different.

Because he would have saved himself...

He'd have made it out with Kami and Cameron, and I'd be the one who was somewhere else, somewhere far, far away...

But things don't always happen according to plan. Life surprises you, it smacks you across the face, and somehow, you're just supposed to smile and keep going.

Well, screw that. And screw life for all its twists and turns.

And above all, screw those three psycho bastards.

# CHAPTER NINETEEN

## *Thiago*

WE MADE IT TO THE UTILITY ROOM. IT SEEMS CRAZY TO say this, but I swear our guardian angel was guiding us. We didn't come across a single soul, and through the exhaustion we could still hear the sound of gunfire behind us. It kept us moving—ready to do whatever it took to make it out of that inferno.

We crisscrossed the halls, climbed the stairs, reached the utility room, and found the ladder. It was big and bulky. Determined as I was, I knew it was practically impossible for me to make it back to the cafeteria with it. I wanted to hide Kam somewhere safe, but I needed her help. I wouldn't be able to move the ladder on my own. And we were doing this for Cameron. We had to get him out of there. There was no way I was going to have the death of another child on my conscience. Not again.

I thought of my sister, who felt closer to me than ever. I could sense her spirit near me—with me—guiding me toward our goal.

This wasn't going to be easy, though. It's one thing to sneak around the halls, careful not to make a sound, but another is to carry something big and heavy to the other end of the building without being noticed.

Before I opened the door, I pulled Kami in tight, told her I loved her, and gave her a kiss.

The look in her pretty brown eyes was the only answer I needed. Her love, her desire for me was all so transparent, I knew I would fight for her.

We walked out carefully, me in front and her behind. I said Lucy's name in my mind and told myself she was watching over us. There was no one in sight. It was eerily silent. Fear and uncertainty were our only companions as we made our way to the cafeteria and then to the kitchen.

"Over here," I whispered to Kami, leaning the ladder against the wall.

She followed me into the pantry, and I climbed up the shelves and pulled away the aprons and rags. A pair of big blue eyes, frightened and teary, looked back at me.

I tried to smile. "I told you I'd be back, right?"

His smile filled me with joy, and I pulled him down when he held out his arms.

"Cam?" Kami asked nervously, standing by the door. Something magical happened when she saw him. Brother and sister reunited, two people who loved each other.

"Are you OK? Did anyone hurt you?" Kam asked, checking him all over.

"I'm fine," Cameron reassured his sister, hugging her as if his life depended on it. And I guess it did.

Trying to encourage him, I said, "Now comes the fun part! Climbing!"

"Like a secret mission?" Cam asked, and I couldn't help but smile.

"Yeah, buddy, it sure is."

We set up the ladder just under the skylight. I'd grabbed a pry bar from the utility room, although I hoped I wouldn't have to struggle too hard to break the glass. After blocking the door with a broomstick—which wouldn't help much but might buy us a few extra seconds in case they came our way—I climbed up, took aim, and hit it as hard as I could. The glass shattered. I cleared out the sharp edges, making sure it was big enough for them to fit through.

"Cam, come on up," I ordered him, staying where I was, knowing I'd have to lift him through the hole. Kam encouraged him, too, and he climbed up carefully and took my hand. I heaved, he caught the edges of the frame, and when he was halfway out and I knew he wouldn't fall, I held on to his feet, pushing him the rest of the way through.

"I'm out," he said.

"You sure are. Now see if you can alert the cops you're up there. I promise you, this will be over in no time," I said, feeling as if a weight had been lifted from my chest.

Now it was Kam's turn, and we didn't have much time. I desperately needed to know she and her brother were safe. "You're not coming with us, are you?" she asked me.

I shook my head, and her eyes, already red, filled with tears as she continued, "Thiago, please…"

"I've got to find him, Kam," I told her. And I knew she understood, and that if her brother were still stuck somewhere inside, she'd do the same.

"Promise me you'll make it out alive—both of you. Promise me," she said.

"I'll do everything I can," I said, kissing her one last time and wishing it was all over, wishing that kiss could go on hours, but there was no time. If the gunmen came in and saw the ladder, we were done for.

I helped Kam climb up, and once they were out of sight, I shouted, "Both of you, get far away from the skylight! See if you can motion to the helicopters or the squad cars! Anything!"

Kam peeked through the skylight again quickly, giving me a look that could have meant a million different things, a million words never said, a million impossible kisses, but there was one thing that shone in her eyes clearly: the memory of us being so happy the night before, making true love, laughing, telling secrets, confessing how much we meant to each other. Despite our fights, despite everything we'd been through, we'd made it that far.

If only I hadn't let her go that morning…

When death knocks on your door, you realize what truly matters and what it means to love someone.

Interrupting these thoughts, a voice came over the intercom. A voice I hated more than any I had ever heard.

"*This message is for you,*" Julian said. "*Yeah, you.*

*You know who the hell you are. I've got your stupid little brother, the one you pretended to love and then stabbed in the back. That's right: Mr. Basketball Team Captain, Mr. Hot Stuff, the asshole who thought he could have his way with my girl and there wouldn't be consequences."*

I heard a blow, followed by a groan.

*"Taylor Di Bianco, do you have any last words?"*

As Kam stuck her head in through the skylight and looked at me with horror, I heard Taylor's voice, his throat dry, his tone agonized: *Get her out of here, Thiago...*

They'd kill him, I knew it. And there was no way I was going to let that happen.

*"Kami,"* Julian went on, *"if you don't come here right now, I'll kill him. And I'll kill his brother, too. And then I'll find your little brother, and I'll do the same thing..."*

When I saw Kami starting to climb back in, I shouted, "No! Get out of here, Kamila. I'll go get Taylor."

"He's going to kill you both, Thiago! I'm the one he wants. I'm not going to stand by and let this happen."

"Goddammit, Kam, no!"

I pulled the ladder away and looked up at her. "Get your brother out of here. That's your obligation. And I'll do the same for mine." I turned around. I didn't want to argue, I didn't want to hear her protest, I didn't want her to feel tempted to jump down. She would do it, she was that brave, or that crazy, and I wasn't willing to risk it. I heard her yelling, "Thiago, no!" But by then, I was already out the door.

It was happening. Now came the worst part.

I didn't have much to defend myself with, just a pry bar and a knife from the kitchen. I knew what I was doing was suicidal, but what other choice did I have? I couldn't leave Taylor there. I wouldn't abandon him. I would stay by his side until the end. That's what brothers do. Strong as the urge was to turn around, climb to safety, take care of Kam, all I could think of just then was my mother, her grief. Losing either of us would kill her.

I had exactly one option, and that was to try. If I gave up now, the knowledge that I had been a coward would haunt me for the rest of my life.

I walked back through the halls. They were silent. How many had died today? How many families would be destroyed?

The question enraged me. My rage was a fire within. I could feel the adrenaline pumping through me, urging me to make a choice.

I might die today. It was likely that I would. But I'd do everything in my power to take those bastards along with me.

# CHAPTER TWENTY

## *Kami*

THERE WAS ONLY ONE THING I COULD DO, AND THAT WAS to get the hell out of there, fast, leaving behind two people I loved like crazy. But I had to save my brother.

I thought about jumping back down into the kitchen, but one look in Cam's terrified blue eyes was enough to realize Thiago was right. I had to get my brother out of here. It was my duty to save him. And when I was done, I'd pray that I hadn't just seen Thiago Di Bianco alive for the last time.

We crawled for a while along the rooftop because I suddenly got scared, imagining there might be a sniper outside. I couldn't help but look through one or two of the skylights as we passed them, seeing rooms where fear had spread into every nook and cranny. The bell rang for the end of first period, making every hair on my body stand on end.

Only forty-five minutes had passed? I felt like we'd been shut inside that living hell all day…

I shuddered. How many kids would never hear that sound again? How many would never again sigh with relief, ready for a break, in search of their friends for some chitchat in the halls? How many people would never again open their lockers to take out their books for the final classes of the day?

These questions were so painful, I didn't know how I'd ever get over it.

"Kami, look!" Cameron shouted, even though I'd told him to be quiet. He pointed at the helicopter on its way toward us, and I felt a wave of relief. I wish I could lie and say I was happy, but all I could think about was the Di Bianco brothers. Who would save them? Who would bring them out alive? I would have gladly sacrificed myself—I knew that was what Julian wanted—but all he'd ever done was lie, so why would he agree to let them go now?

I hated him, and I knew he would never let them out alive.

We waved, blinded by the light of the sun, until the shadow of the helicopter was right over us. They must have been waiting for someone to find a way out.

"Over here!" my brother shouted. "Over here!"

Cam squeezed me tight; I could feel his little heart like a hummingbird in his chest, and his joy was almost contagious. The helicopter hovered low over the roof, and a cop lowered a ladder and climbed down.

"Are you all right?" he shouted. "Is there anyone else with you?" He had to yell over the roar of the spinning blades. I shook my head, and I saw the disappointment on his face. He grabbed my brother in his arms and motioned for me to follow him.

We climbed up into the chopper. Cam's eyes were like saucers as they handed us helmets and earphones and we rose into the air. The school was below us now, the nightmare behind us.

As the policeman looked at me, I started shouting: "What took you so long? Why didn't you do something?" The sorrow, the guilt, the grief, all of that was gone for now, and what I felt was pure rage.

The cop didn't answer, but he looked angry, too. We landed on the football field, and he announced, "I need you to come along. You need to talk to the police chief." From his eyes, I could tell they needed my help. "Anything you can tell us would be useful," he added.

He guided me onto the road that led to the parking lot, where we saw vans, journalists, desperate family members, people crying, hugging, begging for someone to do something. There were ambulances, tents, police cars everywhere, a SWAT team with machine guns. All this, and they couldn't stop three armed teenagers?

I noticed there were lots of students outside hugging their parents and in tears. I was glad so many had been able to escape. They'd survived! That's when I realized this was Julian's revenge aimed at a specific group—me, my friends, and the two loves of my life.

"Over here," the policeman said.

Cam looked up at me and tried to wriggle free, but there was no way I was letting go of his hand.

People saw us and rushed forward, parents and press included.

*"Are there survivors?"*

*"Is Emily alive? Emily Davidson, is she alive?"*

*"Have you seen Harry? My son, Harry?"*

*"How did you get out?"*

They were scaring my brother, who held on to me tight as the cop guided us into the tent.

It was all so fast. I was surrounded by police now, and I wanted to run, not talk. And what was I going to tell them?

"What's your name? Are you wounded?" a woman in a suit asked me, approaching us calmly with a smile on her face.

My brother answered for us. "I'm Cameron, and this is my sister, Kami."

The woman smiled at him, but then looked at me with worry. "Cameron, do you mind if your sister and I talk while my friend takes you to the ambulance to look you over?"

"I'm fine," he said.

"I know. You're a brave little boy. You know that, don't you?"

He nodded.

"Cam, wait for me in the ambulance," I said. "I'll be there in just a second."

"I want Mom," he cried.

The cop who had rescued us from the roof stepped forward and kneeled down. "Come with me, Cam, and we'll get your mom on the phone, sound good?"

My brother looked at me, I nodded, and the cop took his hand and led him away. I wanted to run after him; I couldn't lose sight of him again, but I knew they needed me to tell them everything I knew about the situation.

"You need to go in," I said, staring the woman in the eyes. "Now."

She tried to get me to sit down, but I refused. "What are you waiting for?" I screamed at the whole group, who were all staring at me, dumbfounded.

"We've been told there are hostages. If we go in now, we'll put more lives at risk. Our protocol—"

"Fuck your protocol! They'll kill everyone! My classmates, my best friend—people are getting shot!"

My voice cracked, and I stumbled. My legs couldn't hold me up anymore.

"It's going to be all right," the woman said, trying to calm me down.

"You don't understand!" I screamed. "They don't care about anyone! They'll kill every person in there if you don't go in now!"

"How many shooters are there?"

"Three," I answered.

By the shocked look on her face, I could tell they had literally no idea what was going on inside. "Tell Montgomery what she just said," she ordered one of her colleagues. Then, addressing me, she went on, "I need you to tell me everything. Everything you've seen, everything you know."

And I did. I told her Julian was behind this, and he'd implicated his sister. That Jules had a website where other deranged psychos like him could connect. I told her what had happened a few weeks ago, how we'd figured out he was pretending to be someone completely different, how he was obsessed with me, how they'd found his room full of photos and videos of me and my stuff, and how no one had done anything. I told her he had disappeared, and then we'd seen him the night of the basketball game. I told her about his announcement over the intercom from the principal's office, addressing the students and reading out the list of people he wanted dead. I gave her details of things I'd seen with my own eyes, boys and girls who'd been shot at the hands of those bastards. I said they had tricked my little brother into locking the doors to the gym and cafeteria and how Thiago had broken a skylight to set us free. I told her my best friend was likely dead. I told her I was the one he wanted.

The captain listened to everything I had to say, without interrupting. I added, "If you don't go in now, there won't be anybody left to save."

The woman stared me in the eyes for a few seconds, then turned to her team and said, "To hell with protocol. We're going in."

And that was when the insanity began. Everyone was in motion, while the woman got into an argument with a big-bellied man in a suit jacket. I tried to hear what they were saying.

"You can't—" he told her.

Before he finished the phrase, she said, "The hell I can't." Then she hurried back over and asked, "Where exactly did you say your friends were?"

With all the hope I could muster, I told her, "They're in

the principal's office. Julian's there, too, I'm sure of it. He has Taylor with him. He's waiting for me to show up."

She nodded, and I heard commotion outside the police tent. It was my mother and Ms. Di Bianco struggling to get in.

"Mom!" I shouted.

I ran to her the way I used to when I was a little girl, when she'd wait for me outside daycare and the sight of her would fill me with joy because I knew it was time for us to go home for my after-school snack.

She hugged me, and I buried my head in her arms, and I cried—finally letting out the tears the way I'd needed to all day.

"Kamila, where's your brother?" she asked, terrified. "Where is Cameron?"

"He's fine. The medics wanted to check him over, but he's OK. He doesn't have a scratch on him."

She was relieved, and from the way she was holding me, I could tell she'd just had a brush with the worst fear of her life. She had looked directly into hell, and at the last minute, she'd been released from it.

"My little girl," she said. "It's gonna be OK."

"Kamila, where are my boys? Where are they?" cried Ms. Di Bianco.

Eyes full of tears, I confessed: "They're inside. Thiago got my brother and me out, but he wouldn't come with us, he said he had to find Taylor."

"Oh God," she moaned, covering her mouth to muffle her sobs.

I looked over at the captain, who had been watching the scene in silence. She was looking at Ms. Di Bianco, and once she had our attention, she spoke: "Ma'am, I promise you, I'll do everything possible to get your boys out of there alive."

And unlikely as it seems, I believed her.

I had to.

My mother hugged me tight, and just as we started out to find Cam, a cop sprinted inside the tent.

"Someone else has escaped through the roof, Captain," he told the woman who had just promised me the impossible.

Nervous, but with a glimmer of hope, I watched as Mrs. Di Bianco asked desperately, "Do you know who it is?"

"No, ma'am, we'll find out soon enough."

I wanted to run out and discover for myself that Thiago had made it out safely, that he'd managed to come after us.

But instead, I looked to the tent door and prayed in silence.

*Please God, let it be him.*

*Please.*

# CHAPTER TWENTY-ONE

## *Taylor*

I COULD HARDLY BREATHE. I'D BEEN BEATEN AND KNOCKED unconscious, and when I managed to open my eyes, they just started at it again.

Julian stood there leaning against the principal's desk, watching with satisfaction as his two attack dogs tried to kill me. But I wasn't dead yet. Why hadn't they just finished me off with a bullet to the head?

As I thought this, I looked over at the body of Principal Harrison. His eyes were open wide, lifeless, witness to the whole school descending into horror.

"When you joined in that day as everybody was beating me up, I swore to myself I'd kill you," Julian said, interrupting my frantic thoughts—thoughts that were growing cloudier as pain crept into every inch of my body. "You cool kids think you have the right to do or say anything you want. Your teachers tweak your grades because God forbid you get kicked off the team! The principal overlooks your bullshit. The other students treat you like gods. And why? Because you can throw a fucking ball into a basket?

"Ever since I started school, I was always the best in my class: straight A's. I thought people would admire and respect me for it, but no. Let me tell you a little story about how everybody treated Julian."

As he said this, he bent over and grabbed me by the hair, forcing me to look into his eyes. I didn't say anything. I just listened. That was all I could do.

"You know what they used to do to me when I was ten and I was the smartest kid at school? They'd pick me up," he continued, "and stuff my head in a toilet. Go on, try to imagine that, Taylor. The smell of shit in your hair, feeling it in your nose, in your mouth. Not being able to breathe, needing to throw up, and they just keep dunking you in over and over…"

I closed my eyes and asked myself how I could feel pity for him, despite my hatred for everything he'd done.

"It's no picnic," he said, "but I learned my lesson. I transferred schools, I let my grades suffer, let myself slip to getting B's and C's. I noticed that if you fuck up sometimes, people start liking you better. They ask you to be part of their cliques, they laugh about your shitty grades, thinking you're so cool for not caring. That wasn't easy for me, believe it or not. Have you ever tried failing an exam on purpose?

"I figured out another thing: If I worked on my body and joined sports teams, the girls noticed. If you can hit that six-foot mark, grow some muscles, get a six-pack, they smile at you, give you the eye, invite you to parties. Who cares about a guy's brains when you can have a dickhead with a cool haircut and muscles?"

He let my head drop and continued walking around the room, spouting off. I had no interest in his monologue because yeah, sure, I got it. He'd had a hard time, so what? It didn't justify killing innocent people.

"I've always been an observer; I like to watch people. I like to analyze their intentions, their actions, their dreams, see what makes them tick. And I realized if you understand people, you can get what you want. It opens doors for you, you know? Not that it was easy—I must have gone through five schools before I managed to figure out what I had to do to fit in. And then I found myself here at Carsville with you all, and I had to rethink everything again. Take you, Taylor. You're the captain of the basketball team, you're going out with the hottest girl at school, you get good grades, and fuck, you're even headed to Harvard. I haven't seen anyone stuffing your head in the toilet for getting straight A's."

He laughed and paused for a moment. "*You* changed my whole perspective. *You* got me to look at things differently. *You* made me want to be like you. And all of a sudden, there I was, just another dumbass trying to copy the popular guy. In what universe does it make sense that I would want to be anything like you?"

With no warning, he kicked me in the chest, knocking the breath out of me. "Oh, I'm sorry, Taylor. Did that hurt? I guess you reap what you sow, as the saying goes."

He kicked me again, and I wondered how much longer my body could hold out.

"Why don't we just off this loser?" one of his henchmen asked, a guy I think I'd heard Julian refer to as Rapper.

"Good question," Julian responded, nudging my head with his foot. I didn't have the strength to fight back. I'd already given it a shot, fighting tooth and nail when they nabbed me crossing the main hallway by the stairs, but now there was no point—not when it was three against one, and not with a gun to my head. "You know why I haven't killed you, Taylor?"

I didn't answer him, and in the silence, I heard noise from outside. We looked toward the door, and Julian answered his own question: "Here it comes. This is why I haven't killed you yet."

"Let him go, Jules," Thiago shouted. My brother's voice momentarily made me forget how much pain I was in, but the feeling didn't last long, not long at all. Because I knew exactly what would come next.

"No!" I screamed, but Julian kicked me in the face again.

The metallic taste of blood filled my mouth.

"Let him go," my brother insisted again.

My eyes were practically swollen shut, but I managed to see Rapper and the other guy pointing their guns at my brother.

Why had he come back? Why would he crawl into the belly of the beast when it was almost impossible that he'd make it out alive?

*Because he'd never leave you to fend for yourself, that's why*.

Julian laughed. "Why in the hell would I let him go?" He walked over to Thiago like a lion stalking his prey.

"Take me instead. I'm the one you want," Thiago said, raising his palms to show he wouldn't put up a fight.

"Why would I let one of you go when I can have you both?" Julian asked with a grin.

"For one simple reason," Thiago responded. "Kate."

Julian froze when my brother mentioned his sister's name. Even from my position, lying on the floor, I could tell that the atmosphere had grown tense.

"Where is she?" Julian asked, balling his fists.

"Wow. I didn't expect that reaction, I have to admit. But now I know we're tied. I'll trade you, your sister for my brother. And let's be honest, Jules, the person you really want to put a bullet in is me, not Taylor."

"What makes you so sure of that?" Julian asked in an icy tone.

"Because the girl you're so sickly obsessed with is in love with me, and you don't know how to deal with it. That's why you're here, right? Because for once, you had everything you wanted, and you thought you had the perfect girl in your hands, and then she goes and falls in love with the very opposite of everything you were striving for. I mean, what do I have going for me? I didn't finish college, I don't have a fancy job, and I was on the verge of going to jail. When Kam fell for me, your whole world stopped making sense, because all of a sudden you had to admit that no matter what you did, no matter what your grades were or how popular you got or what team you were on, it didn't matter, because the problem is you. *You're* the problem. There's something wrong inside *you*. And there always will be."

"Shut your mouth and tell me where Kate is," Julian demanded, clenching his teeth. "Tell me where she is or I'll pull the trigger right now!" He aimed the pistol directly at my head.

My brother smiled. *Dammit, Thiago!* I thought.

"Let Taylor go and you'll get me and Kate. That's the deal, take it or leave it."

I knew his plan wouldn't work. Julian was incapable of love. He was incapable of empathy, grief, or remorse.

"No deal, Di Bianco," he said, taking aim at my brother's head. And just then, just as I thought I would see him murdered before my very eyes, we heard a boom coming from outside, and all of us jumped. After that, everything was lightning quick. Someone yelled, "*Police!*" And even though my senses were sharpened in my struggle to survive, it's still hard today to remember exactly what happened.

There were two shots, then they entered the principal's office. Then my life did a complete one-eighty, and everything I loved disappeared before my eyes.

My brother…

My brother lay on the ground bleeding from his head, because that evil bastard, that son of a bitch, had decided to kill himself, but first, he wanted to take my brother with him.

I dragged myself to him as best I could, despite my broken ribs, through the nonstop gunfire, desperate and out of control, but a bubble of calm seemed to form around us.

None of the three killers made it out alive, but they got what they wanted: They'd taken the lives of boys and girls, teachers and children, and they hadn't thought twice about it. As soon as we'd walked in the doors that morning, we were all doomed; there had been no sympathy, no mercy. Those assholes came in and filled the halls with blood, screams, and terror—then took the easy way out. Taking a bullet could never come close to the pain they caused. And there I was, all alone. It would be years before I could close my eyes and get a good night's sleep again.

It wasn't just innocent lives they had stolen. They had stolen my big brother.

The guy who had always protected me, the boy who'd jumped the creek first to offer me a hand when I was scared to cross on my own. The guy who had taught me to play ball, how to smoke a cigarette behind our mom's back, and given me a high five the first time I kissed a girl. I remember how he used to smile at me, encourage me. He would always tell me, *Taylor, once you get going, there's no one in this world who can stop you.* He made the best macaroni and cheese I've ever had. He beat me at arm wrestling a million times. He'd gone to every one of my games to cheer me on even after he'd given up his dream of playing pro. The guy who took over when our father disappeared, and did everything to make sure I still had a good father figure.

My brother.

Thiago.

# CHAPTER TWENTY-TWO

## Kami

I COULDN'T HELP BUT FEEL DISAPPOINTED WHEN I FOUND out the person they'd rescued from the roof was Kate. They brought her into the same tent as me. She looked terrified, and all I could do was scream on the inside. Nothing else could be done by that point: I'd told them everything I knew, everything I'd seen, everything I thought was going to happen.

"What's your name?" the captain asked her when they sat her next to me, wrapped in a blanket.

Thiago's mother looked at her with pleading eyes, as if she might have all the answers.

In a desperate voice, I asked Kate, "Did you see them? Did you see Thiago or Taylor?"

The captain cut me off: "Miss Hamilton, let me be the one—"

"He saved me," Kate said, looking at her hands.

"Who?"

"He told me there was a way out. He asked me... He asked me to tell you..."

"Who, Kate?!"

"Thiago." She looked me in the eyes. "I'm so sorry, Kami. I didn't want—I didn't want to hurt anyone."

She looked at Thiago's mother, who was listening in silence, and started crying and trembling, on the verge of a panic attack.

"Call a medic!" the captain shouted.

"Wait!" Kate said, wiping her face. "He asked me some stuff. He said he needed to buy some time, stretch things out for as long as possible until the police could get inside."

"I told you!" I said to the captain. "They have to hurry!"

"Kamila," she replied, "I already gave the order. Did he tell you where they'd be?"

Kate nodded. "They're in the principal's office. Second floor on the right, behind the staircase that leads to the laboratories."

The captain stood, walked over to her agents, and picked up a walkie-talkie, saying, "We've confirmed the perps' whereabouts. They're on the second floor."

"They won't get there in time," Kate observed.

"Why?" I asked, grabbing her arm and forcing her to look at me.

"I told him. I told Thiago. My brother doesn't care about me. Using me to threaten Jules so he'll give up Taylor would never work."

"Was that Thiago's plan?"

Kate nodded.

"Oh my God," Ms. Di Bianco said, trembling and stifling her sobs.

"I told him to come with me, Kami, I promise I did, but he refused. He said there was no way he'd leave his brother there. He told me—he told me to tell you he loves you, and please forgive him."

I could barely see through the blur of tears rolling down my cheeks, and that was when we heard the shots. First there were just two, sounding much farther away than the shooting had when we were still inside the building.

"No!" I screamed, running out of the tent toward the school I'd attended since I was a little girl, but that was when someone grabbed me and held me back.

"Get her out of here; it's too dangerous," one of the cops yelled.

I could hear Ms. Di Bianco screaming to get through. All she wanted was to feel closer to her boys, but there was nothing we could do except wait. It was like a war zone, with police holding pistols, shotguns, assault rifles.

I heard a voice coming through a walkie-talkie. "They're down. We got all three of them, sir."

Finally, I could breathe. I could breathe a little better knowing it was over. They had gotten them.

"You're confirming, the premises are secure?" one of the cops asked.

"That's affirmative, sir."

The police chief motioned for the other officers to move in, then shouted, "Get that ambo over here. We have two boys in serious condition, one with a gunshot wound!"

My whole world seemed to come to a halt. My life was on the line.

"No," I whispered. "No…"

The officer who had been holding me loosened his grip as he felt me go slack. My strength was gone. I heard the radio. I heard the words of the officer inside, telling his boss what he saw.

"There are bodies everywhere, sir. This is…" The police officer's voice trailed off, and I felt like I was dying.

I kept my eyes glued to the front door. Thiago's mother was crying, but I could barely hear her. I didn't care about the parents trying to push through the line of police, demanding to go in and look for their children.

That's when I saw the paramedics pushing two stretchers through the front door, rushing toward the ambulances. I saw Thiago, shouted his name, and ran up to him, jerking away from the officer behind me. Then I screamed, "Oh my God!"

He was bleeding, badly. His eyes were closed, his body was slack, I would have sworn he was dead, but if so, why was he still bleeding?

"Is he all right?" I asked. "Is it serious?"

"Stand aside!" a paramedic ordered me.

Thiago's mother reached us and screamed, "No!"

He'd been shot. In the head. He wouldn't make it. There was no way he would make it.

"That's my son! That's my boy! Let me through, I need to see him!" Ms. Di Bianco shouted. And finally, they let her through. As she climbed into the ambulance with her older son, she looked back and said, "Kami, you have to look after Taylor."

I nodded, half blind with sorrow, my heart beating out of my chest.

"Bullet wound to the left side of the cranium. Pulse is weak," I could hear the paramedic shout right before the ambulance door closed.

*Bullet wound to the left side of the cranium.*

How could this be happening?

I almost jumped in front of the ambulance, I was so desperate to get inside, but that was when I heard my name—someone calling out to me in a weak and desperate voice. I turned and saw another stretcher, this one with Taylor, beaten so badly I hardly recognized him.

"Taylor!" I ran toward him, crying.

"Kami, my brother... My brother..."

"He's alive, Taylor." That was all I knew, the one thing I could hold on to, and Taylor needed to know that, too.

The medics hurried Taylor into another ambulance. I begged them to let me go along, but they insisted, *"family only."* "He's alone!" I screamed, but they ignored me, leaving me there. I took a deep breath to try and control my thoughts and turned around to see what was going on. I heard screams—screams everywhere. Crying. Sirens. Ambulances coming and going, journalists, photographers, cameramen trying to get comments.

*"How many other survivors are there?"*

*"Did you know the killers?"*

*"Was that kid your boyfriend?"*

My head was spinning, and at one point I looked up and saw helicopters filming. They were already making a story out of it. Trying to be the first to put our tragedy out there in the world.

Paramedics carried the wounded out, and people in hazmat suits were going in. How many people had lost their lives? Everything started spinning...

I heard a shout: "Kami!" I turned and saw Cameron. Something happened inside me: My bones seemed to melt, something told me *now you can rest*, and darkness clouded my eyes as I hit the ground and my body took the rest it so sorely needed.

*Please, God*, I thought. *Please, God, don't let me wake if he's not here with me.*

After that, I remember nothing else.

———

I woke up in the hospital. My brain played a trick on me. For a moment, I thought I was in my bedroom with the same silly problems as always: Did Taylor still hate me? When could I hang out with Thiago again? How would I do on my physics exam?

Then I saw where I was. I scanned the room, recalling everything that had happened, and I felt my chest clench with the same pressure as earlier, but more intensely now, because I knew Thiago's life was on the line, and Taylor was badly wounded.

I sat up and felt a sharp pain in my arm. An IV. I tore it out and started to get up.

"What are you doing?" my mother asked, walking in. "Kamila, you can't do that!"

"Where is Thiago? Where's Taylor?" I asked desperately, ignoring my mother's efforts to pacify me.

"They're being operated on—both of them," she replied with concern on her face.

She looked like she'd aged ten years. Her eyes were red and swollen, and that meant she'd been crying. I couldn't help but assume things were worse than she was letting on.

"Mom, I need you to be honest with me. What's going on?"

"Nothing, Kami. Just relax, OK? I was with Ms. Di Bianco. A neurosurgeon is working on Thiago. The bullet didn't pass directly through the brain, and that's good news, but the operation will take hours."

"Where is he? I want to talk to his mom," I said, now standing face-to-face with her. She must have known it was pointless to stop me, so she led me to the waiting room. Katia Di Bianco, whose own daughter had died in her arms years before, was sitting there, praying that a couple of deranged murderers hadn't taken her two sons' lives.

When she saw me, she called my name and stood to hug me tight. I could feel her body trembling against me. "Are you all right, honey? I saw you pass out."

"I'm fine. How's Taylor?" I asked, despising the world for being a place where hatred, evil, and violence existed. My voice was bitter—how could a tragedy like this happen?

"They're operating on him. He has two broken ribs and a hematoma, but they said he's going to be fine in a couple of weeks. Thiago, though…" She burst into tears and let out a deep sob.

As a reflex, my eyes filled with tears, too, but I managed to reassure her: "He'll be all right, Ms. Di Bianco. Just you wait."

"God willing," she said, looking over my shoulder. "Your mother's so lucky to have both kids alive and well."

I felt terrible, almost ashamed that I had made it through unscathed, and I wanted to run away, flee that terrible reality. It felt like I was on a train, speeding faster and faster, and the only thing I wanted to do was get off before it crashed.

My mother was holding my brother, who had fallen asleep in her arms. It was a crime for a boy so little to have to see the things he'd seen.

Ms. Di Bianco couldn't lose another child. We couldn't lose Thiago now, not when there were still so many reasons to live, so much for me and him to share…

Not even twenty-four hours had passed since we'd been in bed together, wrapped in each other's arms, kissing, exploring each other's bodies, giving each other pleasure and starting to truly love one another—because when that happens, you can feel it. You know it's real. You know this is the person you're meant to be with, you can sense the trust taking root deep within your heart, real, palpable.

I had felt that, I had seen our future, and I didn't need to go out with him for years to find out all the little details about him, his best virtues and worst defects, because I already knew him.

Because he was my missing half, my soulmate—call it what you want. He was the one who had made me the happiest girl in the world, the one who drove me crazy, who had consoled me in the bottomless pit of pain, protected me, and given himself to me, body, mind, and soul, and you know how I knew this?

Because I was the very same for him.

We sat in the waiting room for hours. First, they told us about Taylor. The surgery had gone well, and they were bringing him out of anesthesia. He would need to rest, but he'd soon be back on his feet.

I was relieved. They took us back to see him. He was breathing on his own, he was battered and bruised, but he was still Taylor, my Taylor, my best friend.

Thiago, though... A doctor told us he'd gone into cardiac arrest, but they'd managed to revive him. His life was hanging by a thread, and they hadn't finished his operation yet.

For ten hours, they tried to save him. Ten hours to stop the blood loss, extract the bits of bone lodged in his brain, and remove the damaged tissue. They told us he'd been lucky: The bullet had traveled partway along the bone and hadn't penetrated the skull very deeply. They had performed what they called a decompressive craniectomy, which meant they removed a section of bone to keep the brain swelling from killing him. The surgeon, looking exhausted from so many hours' work, continued, "The upcoming days will be crucial. If the inflammation goes down, we can replace the bone. After that, it's wait and see."

"So he'll get better, right?" Ms. Di Bianco asked the doctor, looking at him as if he were God come down to earth.

"Ma'am, your son's suffered a very serious injury. An injury of this type has about a 5 percent survival rate. Most of those who don't die immediately don't make it long once they enter the emergency room. Your son's strong; he's held on through ten hours of surgery. He's young, too, and he's in excellent shape, so that's not to be underestimated. His blood pressure and his oxygenation levels are in the normal range. He was semiconscious when he arrived, he could squeeze a hand on command when we asked him to, he could blink, and that tells us there is some baseline brain functioning despite the trauma. Trust me, that's a blessing, and the surgery went as well as anyone could have hoped. But this is a very delicate situation, and only time will tell."

Only Thiago's mother was allowed to see him. He spent the next twenty-eight days in an induced coma in the ICU. The inflammation went down, they replaced the bone, but his recovery was slow, and those days were hard—the worst days of my life. Not just because of what had happened to Thiago, but also because the whole town was suffering. Carsville was now news across the nation and the globe. Hundreds of journalists descended on us, camping outside the school and outside the homes of the survivors, ready to entertain the world with our suffering. The death count rose over the next few days: the principal, almost the entire staff, and so many students shot in cold blood.

The town was in mourning. The parents, grandparents, aunts, and uncles of the children lost were our shop owners, our businesspeople, our police and firefighters, and so everything was closed. Things would never be the same here.

We had all lost someone. A friend, a brother, a teacher, a colleague. All of us had to walk behind that long line of cars that drove through the center of Carsville to the cemetery.

Sadness bled into every nook and cranny of our town. A population of fifteen thousand—minus the recent losses—had to watch their loved ones be laid in the ground before their eyes. And most of those gone weren't even seventeen. Lives cut short, dreams cut short, all that joy and hope, all those dreams, gone.

I watched as some of my best friends were buried. Lana died two days after the shooting. They operated on her, they tried to save her, but the damage was too great. Ellie had been shot as we ran to escape, side by side. I missed Chloe's funeral—when the time came, I just couldn't do it again.

Their families were torn to pieces. I remember the look on Mr. and Mrs. Webber's faces, the pain. It was so intense, I could never manage to describe it.

I remember the rage I felt when I saw Danny at the funeral dressed in black. He'd been lucky—he'd been suspended when everything happened. He hadn't had to witness what we'd seen, his life had never been in danger, he didn't have to live knowing all that horror. And to think, he had been one of the first to start beating up Julian that day. I couldn't help but feel this was partly his fault.

Nothing could ever justify what Julian had done. I knew that, but I guess I had to try to find someone to blame now that the person who had truly been responsible was gone. When they'd buried Julian, people had gone to the funeral to scream at his grave. The police had shown up to keep a riot from breaking out.

I hoped he was burning in hell.

The days were brutal, the weeks seemed endless. Every day there was another funeral. All the loved ones who were gone deserved our mourning, our farewells, our words of recollection about their lives.

My father hurried home as soon as he heard the news. He stayed with us, sleeping on the sofa, making us dinner, trying to do whatever he could to help us recover.

We didn't take Cam to any of the funerals. We tried to keep him distracted, and when Dad left, my grandmother took care of him. Cam couldn't really comprehend everything that had happened. Luckily, Thiago had kept him clear from the real horror. My brother hadn't witnessed any deaths, and that helped to preserve his innocence. Still, Cam was never the same person again.

When I wasn't at someone's funeral or consoling someone's family, I was visiting the brothers at the hospital. They still wouldn't let me back to see Thiago, so I would sit in the waiting room for hours, praying for him to open his eyes and smile. Then I'd go see Taylor, until he was eventually discharged a few days later.

We cried together. We held each other in his bedroom, trying to figure out how to process what we'd seen and lived through, trying to get over all the goodbyes we'd had to say.

He was on crutches, and in a great deal of pain, but he went to every funeral he could, every memorial at every church.

We saw psychologists, talked to the police, gave statements to the press. Parents called us, looking for answers, hoping for consolation to ease their suffering. We did what we could. We wanted to help, and we both felt guilty because we'd survived.

It was hard when we saw the images on TV, heard the names of the victims read out, watched the interviews with parents crying in front of the cameras, wanting answers, wishing there was someone still alive they could blame.

The three perpetrators were identified as Julian Murphy, Raphael Vantinsky, and Lucas O'Donnell. All of them were minors, and no one knew where they'd gotten hold of the weapons or ammunition employed in what would be known as the Carsville High Massacre. Who would have been so careless, so heartless, as to sell pistols and high-powered rifles to a bunch of minors? All over the press, all over the internet, people argued over the same endless debate on gun control I'd heard since I was a child.

Should I have spoken up? Maybe. But at that moment in my life, there was only one thing that mattered to me: that the love of my life would open his eyes and smile again.

And so far, there was nothing to hint that it would ever happen.

# CHAPTER TWENTY-THREE

## Kami

WAITING...

I was no good at it. I didn't have the fortitude. If you'd asked me before, I'd have said I was patient. I was a calm person who was mentally prepared to make it through any storm, but this goddamned waiting was killing me.

Thiago wouldn't wake up.

The doctors insisted that the operations had been a success and they could see signs of brain activity, but for some reason, he just wouldn't wake up.

They finally let me see him—his mother wanted me to. I sat there in silence, observing him. A white bandage was wrapped around his head. He was breathing on his own, but he was very still. Very peaceful. He looked like he was sleeping.

His mother kept saying he'd wake up soon, she was sure of it, and I believed her. No other possibility fit into my thoughts. I couldn't bear to think otherwise, I couldn't imagine it.

Thiago *would* wake up.

And yet the days turned into weeks.

Life went on, and I had to make important decisions. A big one was where I would go to school.

Carsville High reopened its doors, but not many of us wanted to revisit those halls; most people didn't even want to walk past the building. Lots of students requested to be transferred to other schools in the surrounding counties. But I outright refused to go at all.

Over Christmas dinner, my father insisted: "Kamila, you have to finish high school."

He had decided to come back to Carsville, at least for a while, to be close to us. And strangely, my mother seemed happy about it. She'd experienced a catharsis of sorts after what had happened, and that changed things for all of us, Dad included. All those hours of not knowing whether we were dead or alive had caused her to rethink many things, and one of them was the way she lived her life.

It seemed like, as a family, we'd found a way to come closer after the tragedy, but quickly my parents seemed to unite against me, and they wanted to decide my future for me and tell me what was right or wrong. I wasn't going to allow that: If I'd learned anything from what had happened, it was that life is a gift, and it can vanish in the blink of an eye. It's far too fragile to spend it worrying about other people's ideals.

"I'll finish school, Dad," I said calmly. "But I'll do it my way."

"Saint Michael's is the best school in the state, and they've offered free scholarships to the survivors. We won't even need to pay for it."

That was another thing: Everyone was showering the survivors with gifts and charity. Famous people had come to visit, colleges were offering scholarships—it was as if none of them realized that the one thing we wanted was to wake up from this nightmare.

"Forget it," I said stubbornly.

My father smacked the table so hard that Mom, Cameron, and I jumped.

"You will! You'll finish school and you'll go to college! Those murderers may have ruined this town, but I'm not letting them ruin your future, too!"

But my life *was* ruined. I felt soulless, only capable of going through the motions: eating, sleeping, doing a little exercise, and not much else.

I didn't want to go to the psychologist.

I didn't want to go to work.

I didn't want to do anything except visit Thiago in the hospital.

That was my life.

Visiting him and keeping him company.

I didn't even talk to him. I'd just sit in a chair and stare.

Day after day, that was all I did, and that was all I wanted to do until he opened his eyes.

"Taylor's going to be studying at home starting in January," my mother said. "Ms. Di Bianco told me. The district has set up a program. You can follow your own schedule, and that will allow you to graduate on time..."

That was another thing.

I didn't want to see anyone.

Anyone at all.

Not even Taylor.

I couldn't look him in the eyes without feeling guilty. I couldn't be around him when deep down I felt partially responsible for what had happened. I had been friends with Julian. I should have figured out he wasn't normal. I should have seen his dark side. Worst of all, both brothers had warned me. Both of them knew, both had tried to tell me, but I hadn't wanted to listen.

And now one was physically and psychologically damaged, and the other—who knew what would happen to him.

"I don't like that idea," Dad said. "Kami hasn't gotten into Yale yet. If her grades drop, her chances could be out the door. I'm not sure they'll think too highly of studying from home."

"I'm not interested in going to Yale, Dad," I said, putting my fork down and staring into his eyes. "Do you honestly think I give a shit about college when the person I love is lying in the hospital in a coma?"

"I know, Kamila, but life goes on," he responded.

"Not for me. When he wakes up, that'll be a different story, but for now, there's no way I—"

"He's not waking up!" my father shouted, making me freeze. When he saw the look on my face, his expression softened, and he tried to grab my hand, but I withdrew it. He went on, "I'm sorry, I'm not trying to be insensitive or tell you to give up hope, but the chances that he'll awaken from a coma after this long are minimal."

"He'll wake up," I said, feeling my pulse start to race. "I know he will, and when he does, I'll be at his side, waiting."

I didn't let them tell me anything else. I didn't care that it was Christmas. I got up and locked myself in my bedroom.

Nobody was going to force me to leave him. I wouldn't let them.

Never.

———

I ended up doing remote school. They sent my brother to Saint Michael's. Every morning, he dressed up in his little blue uniform and left with a smile. He said his new school was *the coolest*.

It's amazing how children can be so resilient in the face of trauma. Cam hadn't seen the worst of what went on at our school that day, unlike Taylor and me, but it was more than enough for a lifetime.

Taylor came to see me almost every day once he got out of the hospital, and that first week, we told each other everything we had to say, but once the funerals were all over, I let him know I needed space. Now we only saw each other at the hospital, when one of us was coming to watch over Thiago and the other was leaving. We had made a schedule—the three of us—so he would never have to be alone.

If I'd been able to choose, and my parents had let me, I would have spent every day and night with him.

And yet, strangely, in all those hours I passed at his side, I never could tell him anything.

I could hardly even open my mouth. I could only look. I looked as the hands on the clock ticked by, and the time came for me to go. I couldn't say anything aloud, but in my heart, I was screaming.

The worst part was watching his body deteriorate. He started to grow a beard after always being clean-shaven, and the nurses made sure to comb his hair, which was so unlike his normal, tousled look. He would have hated that, I thought. His athletic physique started to lose muscle mass. Physical therapists came and went, but there wasn't much they could do, and eventually they had to move him to a rehabilitation facility.

When they announced that, my heart broke, and I realized maybe we really never would get him back. His mother was suffering, but she smiled whenever we crossed paths. She had this idea that if I kept visiting him, he would open his eyes, and I wanted to believe that, too. I wanted it so bad, it was all I could think about, all I could live for.

After a while, Taylor stopped coming so often. It hurt him to see Thiago like that. He told me so one afternoon when he invited me for some coffee at the facility cafeteria.

"You've got to get on with your life, Kami," he said, squeezing my hand. "I don't want to watch you fade away, too."

He had tears in his eyes. I shook my head.

"He's going to wake up, Taylor. I know he is," I said, trying not to burst into tears as he asked if he could hug me.

"When did we turn into this, Kami?" he asked, his head against mine, his scent surrounding me.

I didn't know what to say. I couldn't cure his broken heart, a heart broken twice over: once by me, and again because of his brother. All I could do was hold him, briefly. Then I left.

The holidays came and went, but time seemed to stand still. I hadn't celebrated New Year's. I didn't want to celebrate anything again. I told my parents I didn't want cookies and cakes, presents, cider, I didn't want to stay up till midnight and toast with champagne, I didn't want anything. All I could think about was how terrible the holidays had been, how they had probably ruined the holidays for me forever, and even the end of the school year, which I had looked forward to as a moment when Thiago and I would no longer need to keep things secret, now meant nothing to me.

My parents understood, and tried to respect my wishes, so I only got one present that year, from Thiago's mother. It was in January, in her son's hospital room. She handed me a small velvet box.

"Merry late Christmas, dear. I know Thiago would have wanted you to have this."

I opened it, and inside I saw the colored bracelet he always wore. The bracelet his little sister had made for him and that he never took off. It was silly, just some plastic beads, the kind of thing I used to make when I was a little girl and try to sell on the sidewalk.

"They had to take it off during the operation," she said.

I smiled as best I could through my tears and said,

"Thank you, Ms. Di Bianco." She slipped it on my wrist and helped me knot it. "I won't take it off," I told her.

She kissed my forehead and left.

———

Winter transitioned to spring, and spring brought final exams.

Studying at home served as a distraction, a way to keep thoughts about Thiago at bay. For a few hours, at least, it usually gave me some relief, and since my only other activity was going to the hospital, my grades were excellent, and a little part of me was happy and felt proud of myself. But of course, I thought of Ellie—of all the times we'd talked about going to college. How we'd dreamed of living in the dorms, going out to parties, meeting guys. The thought of Ellie brought back the thought of everyone else—all of them—friends and acquaintances, people who would never go to college or graduate or grow up, who would never fall in love, who would never do anything. They were dead, dead because three worthless sickos had gotten hold of guns and hunted them down like dogs.

My parents were overjoyed with my grades, and I would start getting answers from colleges any day now. Of course, Mom and Dad couldn't stop talking about Yale. All my life, I had wanted to go there, but now, these hopes were indelibly connected with the worst memories of my life. My parents convinced me to send in an addendum to my applications, an essay describing how I had overcome the difficult experience of the school shooting. It was terrible.

Reliving what had happened, trying to put it down on paper—it was an impossible task. There were no words for what I had seen that day at school, for what I had to face every morning when I opened my eyes. There was no way of describing how hard it was to see the person you're in love with slowly wasting away, day by day. The dictionary just doesn't have words to describe so much pain.

The essays must have worked, though, because I got into three different Ivy League universities.

I remember the envelopes all came the same day. They were lying on the kitchen table when I came home from the hospital one warm afternoon. My parents, who were basically inseparable by that point, were waiting for me to open them, but they had already peeked and were too impatient not to tell me.

"You got into all of them, Kami. Princeton, Harvard, and…"

"Yale," I said, slowly walking over to the table and picking up the heavy envelope with its blue and gold lettering.

"Honey, you did it!" my father said, squeezing me tight. "Annie, go get a bottle of champagne!"

I hugged my father, but I wasn't excited. All I could hear in my head, over and over, was:

*Yale is in New Haven, Connecticut.*
*Yale is in New Haven, Connecticut.*
*Yale is in New Haven, Connecticut.*

I couldn't go so far from home.

"I can't," I said, and my parents fell quiet. My mother stopped in front of the refrigerator door and looked over.

"What do you mean?" my father asked, looking shocked.

I couldn't handle a confrontation—not then, when the reality of knowing I couldn't leave was painful for me, too, upturning everything I had worked for.

My father must have read my mind: "You're not insinuating that…"

"I'll do exactly what I said. Once he wakes up, then—"

"You will do no such thing!" he shouted in a fury. "I've been waiting for weeks, for months, for you to get over this, and I'm not going to let you keep wallowing in self-pity, Kamila. Enough's enough!"

Unable to believe what he was saying, I asked, "What do you mean?"

"You're not going back to that hospital."

I laughed bitterly. "You can't tell me where I can and can't go."

"You are going to college! Do you hear me? You're going to Yale."

"You don't understand!" I screamed. "I don't want to leave Thiago, and I'm not going to."

"I'm going to talk to Katia, Kamila. If you remain this hardheaded, you're going to force me to do something I don't want to do."

That got my attention, and I looked him in the eye. "Katia wants me there, Dad. She agrees with me. She thinks if we keep spending time with him, visiting him…"

"Enough, Kamila!" my mother shouted. "Get over him and get on with your life! He's not going to wake up, sweetheart. He's just not. And someday you're going to look back and realize you threw your future away for nothing."

Her tone had softened, and she was trying to soothe me, but it only made me madder. "You don't know anything!" I yelled back. "Neither of you do!"

Furious, I went to my room, where I cried for hours. And before going to bed, I looked through the window, hoping Thiago would appear, as if by magic. I was waiting for a miracle, for him to open his eyes, ask for me, go home, smile at me from his bedroom window like he'd done so many times before.

But his room was empty.

———

The next day, I got up early, even though I'd barely slept, and went to the rehabilitation facility, ready to spend the whole day there. I sat next to Thiago for hours. At some point, his mother appeared in the doorway and asked me to come out and talk with her.

"Your parents called me, Kam…" she said. Hearing her call me that made my heart ache. "They told me you don't want to go to college."

"I'll go when Thiago's better."

She smiled and hugged me. "You don't know how much it means to me that you believe my son will open his eyes again, Kamila. But I can't let you waste your life."

"Katia, this is my decision. I want to be here. My parents don't understand now, but they will."

She shook her head. "I'm sorry, dear, but I can't let you go on like this."

"But—" I heard the fear in my voice. I felt as if I was drowning.

"Today will be your last visit," she said through tears, but firmly.

"No…"

"Tomorrow, I'm taking you off the visitors' list. I'm sorry, Kami. Doing this hurts me more than it does you, believe me, but it's the right thing to do."

"No, no! Please, no," I begged, taking her hands. "Please don't break us apart. Please. I know I can get him to wake up, I know he will. Don't push me away…" I cried, and my legs gave out. On my knees before her, I went on pleading, but it was no use.

She cried with me, but she made me understand there was nothing I could do.

They were pulling me away from Thiago. They were coming between us. I wouldn't be able to see him anymore. It was as if he had died.

———

I cried for weeks. I cried, shouted, broke things, locked the door to my room, barely spoke with my parents.

I cried until I had no more tears left, and when they were gone, I tried to think of what I could do to keep from losing contact with Thiago. I needed to know how he was progressing, if there were changes or improvements in his condition.

Taylor came to see me, and I cried on his shoulder. He

felt my pain, he understood it, and he cried with me. He had gotten into Harvard, and he was leaving, too. We were both leaving Thiago behind. His mother would bear the burden alone, but she knew Taylor had to live on, had to live for his brother, it was what Thiago had wanted when he'd gone back for him. It was what he'd sacrificed his life for, so Taylor could live out his dreams. Taylor had to live for him. That was what he told me.

When he left, I sat at my desk, looked out the window, and sent an email to the university to confirm my attendance.

When I told my parents, they looked at me as if I'd lost my mind.

"Harvard?"

"Harvard?!"

"Yes, Harvard," I said dryly. It was the first time I'd spoken to them in weeks. "You wanted me to go to college, and I'm going, so you should be happy."

"Why Harvard, though? What happened to Yale?" Dad asked.

I didn't say anything, but my mother's face told me she knew. "It has to do with Taylor, doesn't it?"

I didn't answer, though I was surprised by how quickly she had guessed. I just left the kitchen and went back to my room.

I was going to Harvard because Taylor was my last link to Thiago. If we were at different universities in different states, I'd never know anything about the person I loved except for what his mother would tell me over the phone. And besides, Taylor helped numb my pain, helped me still feel Thiago close. I knew it was weird, maybe even wrong, but I didn't care, and I didn't care what anyone thought: not my parents, not Katia; it didn't even matter what Thiago would have told me to do if he'd been conscious.

When it was time to leave, I packed my bags, despite my feelings of reluctance and disgust. It was emotionally draining to have to close doors I wasn't ready to close yet, say goodbye to a family I hadn't been kind to but that had supported me and helped me keep my head above water all those months.

I asked Katia to let me say goodbye.

My parents understood, and even she eventually agreed to let me see him one more time.

I barely recognized him. Over the spring and summer, he had grown so much thinner. Before, he'd looked like he was asleep. Now it looked as if he was fading away.

I didn't sit beside him like I had done before. Now I stood at the foot of his bed. I observed him in silence, remembering how much I had prayed for him to open his eyes. As I stood there, I became awash in rage, rage fueled by all the pain I'd kept inside.

After a few minutes, I spoke, and my voice sounded unrecognizable. I let out all the things I'd been holding inside. I was furious, I started screaming at him, I wanted to hit him, to hurt him, I wanted him to feel the pain I'd felt when he left me all alone.

"How could you do this to me?" I began. "You promised me you'd be OK! You promised we'd be together! You promised you'd stay by my side, through good and bad! I begged you not to go! I told you to come with me! But no, you had to play the hero, and now look at you! How am I supposed to go on without you? How am I supposed to just go and live my life when I know you're still here, breathing, maybe dreaming? Knowing that even if you're not conscious, you still love me!"

I walked over to him, squeezed his hand, and fell to my knees. My rage died down, replaced by grief. I sobbed—no one could imagine what I was feeling just then, no one but him, perhaps.

"Come back to me, come back to me, please..." I pleaded, my tears filling the palm of his hand. "Come back to me, put an end to this nightmare, make it end, please. I need you. I've always needed you; I've always loved you...even when I was little. Please, don't leave me alone, don't abandon me in this world full of hatred, fear, sorrow, and grief. Please come back."

I don't know how long I was there, crying. It felt like hours. All I know is I got the time I needed to say goodbye— the way I wanted to, the way I had to.

"I'm going to Harvard," I said when I realized it was time to go, when I was tired of waiting for him to open his eyes. "They say I've got to get on with my life, but what they don't understand is deep down I will never stop waiting for you. I love you, Thiago."

I wiped a tear from my cheek and walked out of his room.

There was one thing I didn't see: a slight movement of his ring finger after I had shut the door and left.

# Part Two

—

# DECLINE

# CHAPTER TWENTY-FOUR

## Kami

TWO YEARS LATER

LOTS OF THINGS CAN HAPPEN IN TWO YEARS. SO MANY that our brain tucks half of them away because it's impossible to remember so much. How can I give you an idea of what happened during that time? How can I get you to understand the mistakes I made? All of them guided by the desperate need to move on and get over my pain, which was so profound that for a long time, I could barely breathe.

I went off to college, even though it was the last thing I wanted to do. I left because I was more or less forced to by the people who supposedly loved me and wanted the best for me. Now that time has passed, I understand them, but back then, they felt like enemies to me. I hardly spoke to my parents that first year of college. With Katia, it was different. We had long talks at first; I told her what life at Harvard was like, and she would talk about Thiago and how she was still waiting for him to wake up. But then a moment came when the conversations got shorter and shorter, and I could hear the pain in her voice every time she had to tell me nothing had changed; Thiago was the same.

I had to stop talking to her. It wasn't easy.

And with Taylor, it was even harder. He asked me to stop contacting his mother. He said they could never move on with me pulling him back in. Maybe he was right. Maybe moving on was what we both needed, but for me it felt impossible if moving on meant leaving Thiago behind. I needed to know how he was doing. I needed to keep hope alive. But finally, I erased Katia from my phone and blocked her number, along with anyone who might have kept me informed of Thiago's condition, which was always the same: bedbound, deteriorating by the day. It was hard to stop calling. That was my one tie to Carsville and Thiago. But my hope had died with the waiting and the growing knowledge that I was never going to get that call telling me that something had finally changed.

I needed to take stock of the harm I was doing: to my parents, because I had shut them out; to my little brother, because I couldn't feign happiness when we spoke; to Thiago's mother, because I wasn't letting her heal; and more than anyone else, to Taylor.

Because I did something soon afterward, something I know I can't justify, but my heart, my body, and my mind needed him the way a drowning person needs a breath of air.

We ran into each other one day on campus. He hugged me, and we grabbed a coffee at a little place nearby and talked about everything and nothing, and finally he addressed the elephant in the room: "Kami, why did you decide to come here in the end?"

I couldn't lie to him. I wouldn't know how. "You're the only thing that keeps me close to him..."

The grief in his eyes, the pain my words caused him, were nothing compared to what I was feeling. Or at least, so I told myself then. I had forgotten that Taylor hadn't only lost his brother, he'd lost me as well. I didn't think about his feelings, I didn't consider how a hug from me might remind him of what we once had, and I didn't know that he'd been keeping an eye on me all over campus from a distance, that he'd even talked to my roommate many times to find out how I was.

These are the kinds of things you're not aware of when you're in the state I was in, submerged in your own pain, your own grief, your own thoughts.

We talked for hours, but after that, the distance between us remained. I ignored his messages and calls, closing myself off again, because I couldn't stand to be reminded of that pain. Months passed, but then we saw each other at a party.

I hadn't been going out. My roommate and the friends I'd made had stopped even inviting me. They'd learned to accept me for who I was, or for who I'd become from so much pain, and they respected the fact that I was the kind of friend you could have coffee with or watch a movie with once in a while.

I don't know exactly what led me to go out with them

that night. Maybe I just needed to finally get out of bed, get my head out of the books, get dressed up for once. It wasn't some kind of sign that I was starting to get over what had happened. On the contrary: I was so sad, so desperate, that I needed a distraction to keep me from doing something truly crazy.

I needed to feel again, to feel *him* close, and that's why I went to the party—to find Taylor, to see him again.

Because if I couldn't be with Thiago, I could at least be with the next best thing.

It took me a while to find him. Someone offered me a drink, and I accepted. Then another, and I took it, too. The alcohol helped me relax, the same way it had more than once when I'd stayed in alone, drinking in my room.

Finally, I saw him standing in the opposite corner.

He was smiling.

He was handsome.

There were two girls chatting with him.

It bothered me at first to see him looking so relaxed with all those people around, looking happy even, just being normal when his brother was lying in bed in a coma after saving his life. The thought barely formed before I forced it out of my head.

I had stopped hating the cause of all this; I knew I couldn't blame Taylor for surviving, even if his survival was the reason his brother was unconscious.

He must have felt someone watching him, because he looked around, and finally his eyes settled on me. I saw surprise on his face, but a few seconds later, he smiled.

He cut off the girls talking to him, actually just walked away from them without saying anything, and crossed the room to where I was. When I smiled back, I realized it had been ages since I'd used those muscles in my face; they felt tight, rusty.

"I didn't think I'd ever run into you at one of these parties," he said.

"I feel a little weird being here," I replied, noticing how different he looked. He had let his beard grow out, and his hair was shorter. He was on the basketball team, which explained all the girls following him around.

"I'm glad you got out of the dorm. It'll do you some good," he told me. "What are you drinking?"

"Gin and tonic," I replied. But it was really mostly gin.

He had to struggle to hear me, the music was so loud.

"You feel like going outside?" he asked, and the question reminded me of the good times we'd shared, the sweet caresses, the silly laughter. I nodded, and we walked out onto the porch of the huge frat house.

"How are your classes going?" he asked.

To tell the truth, Harvard was insanely difficult, but since all I did was study, I was getting by. "Not bad, and yours?"

"I'm surviving. But I'm not going to lie to you, I feel like a moron here sometimes."

I rolled my eyes. "Yeah, I'll bet you're really struggling."

He smiled at me again. I think that smile was what started it all.

He took me back to my dorm after the party, told me

how happy he was to see me, and begged me to pick up the phone when he called, and to stop ignoring his messages. He wasn't going to try anything, he swore—he just wanted to be sure I was all right.

I did as he said, and we started talking again; we even hung out a few more times. First for coffee, then for lunch, eventually for dinner. We went back to being the Taylor and Kami from before, inseparable, and right when I thought our friendship had been renewed, that friendship that had brought us so close, that had defined us—he kissed me.

It was a sweet kiss, bringing all the contradictory feelings to the surface.

I didn't stop him—because I liked it. I closed my eyes and let myself feel something again, and for a moment, that was enough. What I didn't expect was what came next.

How his gentleness slipped into something rougher. Hungrier.

We stopped making plans for dinner or coffee. We only hung out to have sex—to fuck—because that's the only word that describes what we were doing.

It was weird. It was as if we were searching in each other for a kind of forgiveness we didn't deserve, because the burden of guilt was consuming us. I felt horrible. I felt like I was cheating on Thiago, like I was the worst person in the world. And that destroyed us.

Our sex turned savage, possessive. So possessive that the Taylor and Kami who had fallen in love with each other once before vanished, replaced by something ugly and desperate.

After the fucking came the fights, the accusations, the jealousy. We both wanted something from each other that we'd never be able to give, because there was too much pain inside of us, and we were tired of swimming against the current.

I never forgot Thiago. I never stopped thinking of him—*he* was the person I saw when Taylor touched me, the one I thought of when Taylor's hands squeezed me tight or brought me to orgasm.

We'd started our second year of college by then, not kids anymore, when without even realizing I was doing it, I started to ask the wrong questions. At first, I was subtle: *Nothing's changed, right? No news?* Then I got more desperate: *Do you think he'll wake up? Have you gone to see him? How does he look now?*

And one day, he screamed, "Drop it!"

That scared me.

"Don't you realize how much you're hurting me, Kamila? What the hell are we? Be honest, dammit, because you're driving me crazy!"

I knew he was right.

He continued, "This has to end. You haven't gotten over him. You say you love me, but I feel like he's the one who's still in your head. And it's not because you're worried about his health, it's because you're so fucked-up over losing him that you don't know how to move on with your life. You're using me to find out about him. Don't you see how twisted that is?"

"Taylor, I—"

"I'm sorry, Kami, I really am, but I need to stay away from you. I need to forget you if I'm ever going to move on. I love you; do you not understand that?"

"I love you, too," I said, and I meant it.

"But you're not in love with me," he interrupted, emphasizing every word, and I had no idea how to respond. "And I get it now. Finally. I guess I always knew deep down, but when we hooked back up, I thought—I don't know, I thought we could save each other somehow. I thought we could be happy together, that I could take care of you and make you smile again, but all we're doing is hurting each other. I don't like it. I don't like the person I've become. You and I aren't made to be together, and as much as it hurts, I think it's time to bring this to an end."

I cried.

Of course I cried, because Taylor was my drug, he helped soothe my pain, and his pulling away destroyed me. He kept his distance. For months, I knew nothing about him, nothing at all, until… Well, until *it* happened.

When I finally went home, it was during the Christmas break of my second year. The year before, I'd spent the holidays in the dorm and enrolled in summer classes, because I couldn't stand the thought of returning to Carsville. Doing so was as painful as I'd imagined. My brother was getting huge, and he hugged me as soon as he saw me and wouldn't let me go. My parents were back together, and I made peace with them. They still fought sometimes, but Cameron seemed genuinely happy.

Despite the tragedy, the town had gotten its winter

charm back, and I walked through the square as if nothing had happened. A closer look revealed the sad truth: When you looked at the faces of the mothers and fathers and realized you couldn't ask them how their kids were, it was devastating. Whoever said time heals all wounds should have seen them. It had been a while since I'd seen Mrs. Mills, and when I finally stopped by the café, I found out her husband had passed. She tried to smile when she saw me, but losing her life partner, the father of her kids, the man who won her heart and made her happy for fifty long years... That had been too much, even for her.

She poured me a giant mug of coffee with a pinch of cinnamon, and we talked for a long time. She asked about my family and about Harvard. By the time I left the café it was night, and snow was starting to fall.

I didn't have an umbrella or even a hat, but I enjoyed the walk. I hadn't known how much I'd needed it. I needed to make peace with the town where I'd grown up, painful as that was, agonizing as it was to look around and be reminded of all the friends I missed so much and would never see again.

I told myself it was finally time to go see Thiago's mother. Katia smiled when she opened the door for me. There was pain in her eyes, but still, she pulled me in for a hug. As soon as I saw her, I knew something bad had happened, and I felt my legs buckle when she used the horrible phrase *withdrawal of care.* She invited me in to sit down as she explained the process to me.

"Taylor says it's time. He says Thiago would never have agreed to live like this for so long, that this isn't living."

"Taylor said that?"

Katia looked at her hands, lost. "I don't know what to do. He deteriorates more and more by the day."

"He's still there, Katia! It's still him! And he'll come back! I know it!"

She shook her head.

I shouted, "You can't just let him die! You can't!"

"If you could…" Katia began, but she couldn't finish the phrase.

I stared into her eyes. "If I could what?"

She shook her head.

"Katia, tell me. Whatever it is, just say it."

"Taylor made me promise not to tell you. He said you were in bad shape and needed to move on. Your parents said you couldn't go see Thiago anymore, and I thought that was for the best. But the last time you saw him, he made clear improvements. He even moved his fingers; he opened his eyes at one point. The doctors told me not to get too excited, they said those were unconscious reactions to stimuli, and it didn't mean he was going to wake up. The days passed, and it didn't happen again, but I thought—I thought it was you who did it. I think he heard you and that made him want to come back."

I can't describe what I felt at that moment. The last time I'd seen Thiago, I'd told him everything, I'd shouted at him, I'd let it all out, thinking he couldn't hear me—but he could… He had.

I had awakened him.

"Mom, are you starting with that again?" I heard

Taylor's voice from the kitchen. I turned and saw him, and he looked upset, angry even. We hadn't seen each other in months, not since we'd broken up, or whatever you'd call it.

"I told you to leave my mother in peace," he told me.

I tried to answer, but Katia did first. "Taylor, Kami is like family."

"She's just going to get you upset!"

I got up from my chair, ready to go, but Katia grabbed my wrist, pulling me back toward her, and yelled at her son in a way I'd never heard her do before. "She's trying to help us! And there's nothing I won't do before I just let my son die!"

Incredulous, Taylor spoke again: "Are you listening to yourself? Kamila can't save Thiago, Mom; she's not a doctor, and she doesn't have a cure for him. Have you lost your mind?"

"I refuse to lose another child!" she shouted, bursting into tears. "If Thiago dies, I can promise you I'll be the next to go!"

Taylor glowered at her, and a few seconds later, he broke the silence: "Then I guess I'll have to learn to live alone. No mother, no brother, no father, no sister. I can't control that. But I'm not going to waste my life."

He turned and walked off, glancing at me for a moment with disappointment in his eyes.

What did he expect me to do?

I agreed with Katia!

I needed to believe there was still a way!

There was, wasn't there? There had to be!

# CHAPTER TWENTY-FIVE

## *Thiago*

REMEMBER THE MOVIE *INTERSTELLAR*? YOU HAVE TO. That amazing Christopher Nolan flick with Matthew McConaughey traveling through space to try to find a new home for mankind. It has all these crazy plot twists and incredible sequences and almost everything happens somewhere far off in the galaxy. When I saw it, I remembered there was one thing that got my attention. It didn't have to do with the plot, per se, it was about this one scene that everybody seems to remember, just one: when Anne Hathaway and Matthew McConaughey are supposed to find Miller's planet, which is orbiting on the edge of a black hole, making time slow down; an hour there is like seven years on Earth. Can you imagine walking on Miller's planet and coming back to find your mother, your children, or your grandkids seven years older?

It would be insane, right?

Well, that's what it was like for me, as if I'd been forced to go spend the night on Miller's planet, as if someone had said, *Get some rest, pal, don't worry about anything, we'll wake you up soon and you can get back to your normal life.*

My normal life?

But why would I go back when I was so comfortable?

Why would I want to leave when I had her with me, by my side?

"You want to play again?"

I opened my eyes, and there she was. Her blue eyes, her blond hair. She was still just five years old, which didn't make any sense, or maybe it did, if I told myself this was how things happened on Miller's planet.

"Again?" I asked, drawing the word out, which made her smile even wider.

"But this time, I get to hide," she said, her eyes wide as she ran off.

"Fine." I smiled. "One...two...three!"

It was an endless pleasure, playing with her again after all those years without seeing her, after thinking I would never see her again.

We had our little routine now, our pattern. For days, we'd been walking around that nameless lake, then eating macaroni and cheese (she never wanted anything else), then playing cards, hide-and-seek, or having tea parties with her dolls. Sometimes, if she was in the mood, we even shot some hoops.

It was like a retreat, and I was enjoying it. I had needed it, I'd needed to make up for lost time with my little sister, the sister who had died so many years ago. I'd never had a chance to say goodbye.

I used the time with her to talk about the day she was taken from us. She could barely remember anything. I cried and begged her to forgive me. She kept asking for Mom, constantly. She told me she missed her, especially when she went to sleep. But otherwise, she was happy where she was.

But where was she?

In my head, it was Miller's planet, but that was because I watched too much sci-fi. We did have to be somewhere, though, right?

Did I ever tell myself we were in heaven? Of course I did. I think that was the first thing that went through my head when I saw her, but come on—where was everybody else? Were we the only ones who lived there, in heaven, in that other world, or whatever you want to call it?

That was impossible.

But since I didn't have answers, I stopped asking questions.

I liked being there. It gave me space to think—and to start healing, even if it was alongside the person who'd made my heart ache in the first place.

Was I dead?

There was a moment when I started to think so. I even started accepting it. But then, why was it that I still had dreams, and why was *she* always in them?

Her, the girl I was in love with. So in love that I kept wanting to go back, even when Lucy was curled up on my lap. At times, I thought I heard her, not often, but I did. Somehow, I always felt her near me.

I could sense my mother and brother, too. I heard Taylor's apologies so many times I knew them by heart. And I wanted to tell him to forget me, that he didn't need to ask for my forgiveness. I was fine, I was with Lucy, I was…happy.

But was I?

Deep down, I think I always knew I could go back, and that's why I was calm. Calm especially with regard to my family, my mother. I knew how much she'd love to hear all about Lucy, how it would ease her soul to know that her daughter was safe and sound.

As for Kam, I could remember one time when she screamed a bunch of things at me. It had only been a few days ago. Or at least, it felt like a few days. I know when that happened, I had really wanted to go back and tell her how I felt. I wanted to apologize for not keeping my word, for letting her down. And I wanted to ask her to wait—just wait for me a little longer.

That was the only time I felt closer to *there* than to here, closer to my life on Earth than on Miller's planet, but the feeling lasted only a second.

Then I stopped hearing her voice.

She was gone.

And it was strange, because her voice was like a thread that kept me connected to my life on Earth, but the thread was getting thinner and thinner, and I started to just want to stay where I was. I was comfortable there, and I had my sister to keep me company.

Earth had given me lots of headaches, I had come up against so many obstacles in my path, and then there was the shooting at school, which had ruined everything. Why should I go back there?

Then I heard her voice—her beautiful voice echoed again somewhere. Or maybe it was all in my head?

*Thiago, please, come back. Come back to me, please.*

I looked up into the sky, and a drop fell on my face.

Did it rain on Miller's planet?

"Those are tears," my sister said.

She had come out of nowhere and taken my hand.

"Tears?" I asked.

She nodded. "They're hers. Kami's," Lucy said, as if she had just seen her the day before, or as if she were seeing her right now.

"How do you know?"

"I just do," she said, shrugging. "She wants you to go back."

At first, I didn't say anything. I just let the rain soak my face, my hair, my clothes, and then I knew it. "It was you, wasn't it?" I asked.

Lucy smiled. "What do you mean, it was me?"

I kneeled and looked her straight in the eyes. "It was you who guided me through the school. It was you who got Kam and her brother out of there. Am I right?"

Lucy nodded.

"I knew I could never be that lucky on my own."

"They shot you in the head," my sister said.

"And yet I'm still alive...here...with you...on Miller's planet..."

"Where?" she asked, laughing.

I didn't reply, and she continued, "This isn't a planet, dummy."

"What is it, then, smarty-pants?" I asked.

After a second without speaking, she answered, "I guess it's just the place you were supposed to be during this time."

I didn't understand what she meant, but I didn't ask for an explanation either. We just watched the rain, quietly sitting next to each other.

"You're going to leave, aren't you?" she asked.

I looked into her blue eyes and hesitated. "I don't know..."

# CHAPTER TWENTY-SIX

## Kami

DESPITE MY PARENTS' RESISTANCE, AFTER ALMOST A YEAR and a half, I gathered my courage and returned to the rehabilitation facility to visit Thiago. His mother was there, and she hugged me when I arrived, hope glimmering in her bright, tearful eyes.

It wasn't easy to return after so much time. It meant stirring up the pain, the tragedy, the loss, remembering dark days when I'd sat next to him, saying nothing, just crying because he wasn't there with me. But the hardest part was walking into his room and seeing the state he was in.

The person lying in that bed didn't look in the least like Thiago. He was sunken and thin—frighteningly so. His face looked like someone else's, and his muscles were gone.

I wanted to take off running when I saw all those machines keeping him alive. I even wondered for a moment whether Taylor had been right, whether unplugging him would be the best thing for him.

What would Thiago think if he could see himself like this?

What would he have asked us, begged us to do, had he known he would be spending years lying in a bed?

I was scared—scared that I might be wrong—scared that what I thought was best for him was just my selfishness speaking.

For a few days, I sat there next to him, not sure what to say. I told him a little about my life, about Harvard, about why I'd decided to go there instead of Yale. It was weird at first, because I felt like I was talking to myself, but it got easier. Soon it turned into a kind of therapy.

The first sign that it was working came fast. Just two days after I started going to the facility, something small, almost imperceptible, occurred. But I saw it: One of his fingers twitched against the mattress.

The second sign, on the seventh day, was when his eyelids trembled.

I told the doctors about both, but none of them seemed surprised or especially hopeful. They told me they had seen brain activity, that they knew he was even dreaming, and his movements could have to do with that. At any rate, it was nothing out of the ordinary, they said.

But I knew otherwise.

It didn't matter what they said. I was hopeful now, excited. When I told my parents I wasn't going back to college that spring, all hell broke loose. My parents even spoke to Katia, but this time, she backed me up.

This was more important than everything else, and I wouldn't leave. I wouldn't stop going to visit until I proved that Katia and I were right and Thiago opened his eyes. He would open them for me, for his mother, for his brother—his will to live was still burning inside him, I knew that. And a life spent in a hospital, being tended to by doctors and nurses, would never be enough for him. He was hungry to live.

Two weeks later, there was too much evidence to ignore—he was changing, and the doctors had to start paying attention. The physician overseeing him explained to us that there were drugs used to try to bring patients out of a coma—they had tried them with him before but hadn't had any luck. Maybe this time would be different. But he told us not to get our hopes up. Reawakening after that long was very, very rare, let alone a full recovery.

It was a slow process, but he responded well. He had spasms and tachycardia, but slowly and steadily, they brought him back to us.

His mother and I were elated. It was working: Thiago could hear me. He wanted to come back. He wanted to come back to me.

I knew it. He had to.

I told him everything. I told him Taylor and I had gone out again for a few months. I told him that our relationship had started off well but had become more and more complicated. I told him I'd been selfish, that I'd gone to Harvard and gotten back with Taylor because it had been my way to hold on to him, Thiago.

It wasn't easy to confess, but I'm convinced that those talks were key in Thiago's recovery, and he finally awoke.

That's right. Thiago woke up.

Two years. Exactly two years passed before Thiago Di Bianco decided to open his eyes.

It was a day like any other, but it was a day I'd remember for my entire life. It was a rainy, cold day. Christmas was around the corner. The third Christmas since the shooting had happened. I was twenty years old now. Time had flown by, but at the same time, it had been frozen, frozen for Thiago, for his mother, for Taylor, for me. Time freezes when the person you love is locked in a struggle between life and death.

I was with him when he opened his eyes, and I'm telling it this way because nothing ended up how I thought.

Was he happy to see me?

Of course he was, although when it happened, he didn't know where he was, or who he was, and he remembered nothing about the shooting. It took him a few days to orient himself, to remember why he'd been in a coma for two years.

It wasn't easy filling in the blanks for him, or watching his reaction when the doctors told him about his brain injury and everything that had happened to his body after being unconscious for so long.

That was when the hard times came, when we started to understand that what had happened to Thiago could have many aftereffects. Too many.

He got frustrated when he struggled to speak, unable to communicate using even the most basic words.

It was difficult to see someone as strong as Thiago going through something like that, and he didn't want me to witness it.

He hardly spoke to me. He said he couldn't find the words, but the nurses told me he was getting better all the time. He would tense up when I visited him. I realized he was uncomfortable whenever I was around. But why? Why would he feel that way?

"Go back to Harvard," he told me during one of his physical therapy sessions. He was so weak that he could hardly stand and take a few steps.

"But I want to be here. I want to help you—"

"I don't!" he shouted, and everyone in the physical therapy room turned and looked at us. "It's killing me, letting you see me like this— I can't. I can't have you close right now. I need you to go."

He was shaking, so the doctors rushed in to assist him. Finally, his mother told me to go.

"Give him time, Kami," she told me in the hospital cafeteria. "He doesn't feel like himself; his body and his brain are betraying him, and he doesn't want you to see him in this state. I know my son, and the same way I knew you would bring him back, I know that right now, you being here is only going to slow down his recovery."

It was hard to accept, and I resisted it at first, but it was true that whenever he saw me, he got worse. As soon as I walked into the room, he'd turn angry and tell me to leave.

I cried all night, and then in the morning, I tried to force a smile.

What was happening? Was I going to lose him all over again? After all the time I waited for him to come back to me?

I didn't know, so I decided to return to Harvard.

The day before I went back to school, I visited him in his room.

"I'll wait for you," I told him. He looked better, a little more like himself even though he was still so thin. They'd given him a shave and styled his hair like before, but he was far from that athletic guy he'd been. His vitality was missing.

He was staring out the window, looking irritated. I didn't get it. I didn't get why it was so hard to look at me.

"I was with my sister," he confessed finally, and it was the first time in days he'd said something to me that wasn't a complaint or dismissal.

I froze. "What... What do you mean by your sister?"

"I mean the only sister I have, the one I lost. I was with her, I could see her, I could hug her, I could run around with her and play hide-and-seek. We talked, and that pain tucked so deep inside of me—I felt it disappear."

I stood there waiting for him to continue, not knowing what to say, because we both knew his sister was dead. If he had been with her, did that mean Thiago had been dead, too?

"You brought me back, and I'm thankful, but sometimes... sometimes I wonder if that was what was supposed to happen. Is this really the place for me after everything that happened?"

"Your place is wherever I am, isn't it?" I asked, trying with all my strength not to burst into tears.

His green eyes looked straight into mine.

"I don't even know if I'll fully recover. I don't know if

I'll be able to walk like before, or run, or play basketball. I don't know if my body will ever be the same. And you deserve better."

"I deserve to be with you," I said.

"No! You deserve to be with someone who won't be a burden to you. You deserve someone healthy, strong, mentally capable, someone who can give you everything you deserve. And me—"

"You're going to get better."

"I need you to go, Kamila," he said, and when he called me by my full name, I always knew he was serious. "Don't make me repeat it. I won't let you throw your life away because of me."

I was furious. Didn't he realize how much I had suffered? Was he aware of the mental and emotional effort I had made coming to see him every day, drawing strength from places I didn't know I had to will a miracle to occur? And this was how he thanked me?

I stood. "I think I deserve a lot more than this," I responded, holding back my tears. "Do you have any idea how much—"

"I didn't ask you to," he cut me off again. "I'm grateful for your efforts, for your hope and commitment. I know you were determined to wake me up, but I can't just pick up where we left off. I can't look you in the face knowing I don't deserve you. So please, just go, start your life over, because I have a long road ahead of me, and I have to walk that road alone."

Alone?

I left feeling rejected and wounded—my whole body was heavy with pain.

I didn't understand why he wouldn't let me be there for him.

But I gave him his space.

I went back to college and left behind the depressive Kami, the weak Kami, the Kami who stayed in her room reading stories of people who had awakened from comas and learning about the aftereffects of brain trauma.

I became myself again, left the pain behind, hard as it was—and it was the hardest thing I'd ever done—but I couldn't go on sacrificing my life for others.

I had done my job; I had fought for him, for us. If he didn't want to see it that way, and this was how he thanked me, then maybe, maybe I had been wrong.

# CHAPTER TWENTY-SEVEN

## *Thiago*

I DIDN'T RECOGNIZE MYSELF. WAKING AND SEEING HER there... It was the most wonderful thing that could ever have happened to me. But nothing works out the way you expect, and nothing is so simple, especially not when you wake up after being in a coma for two years.

Two years!

Fuck, it felt like two days for me. I was disoriented and lost at first, but then the memories came back in sharp detail, and I remembered how it all had gone down: the shooting, the fear, the desperation, the need to get Kami and her brother out of there, the risk I ran when I went back inside to save my brother. I knew it was impossible, practically a suicide mission, but it had worked—or almost.

I had made peace with the fact that going back in there would mean my death. I knew it would be frightening, and I knew someone would end up hurt, but if I could save Taylor's life, that would be worth it.

But I never thought I could get shot in the head and survive, let alone spend two years in a coma.

Kam was different now. The way she looked at me was different. She was an adult now, an adult who had seen too much. She was hiding so much pain, it was hard to be around her. She looked the same, but she had lost the innocence and tenderness of the girl who used to look at me through her bedroom window.

I loved her. Dammit, I loved her like crazy, but when I looked at myself and the person I'd become, all I felt was contempt.

It was hard to look in the mirror and see my body so ravaged. I was so pale and skinny, I didn't even recognize myself in my own reflection. But that was the least of it. The worst thing was losing control over my body, feeling clumsy, freezing up, not finding the right words to express myself. My brain was still asleep somehow, lethargic, dazed, and I thought it would never be the same.

I started reading up and talking to the doctors to try to understand what was going on. They told me to be hopeful, that with time and rehab, I could be the person I used to be, *probably*. They never quite promised it, and if I couldn't get back to one hundred percent, I didn't feel capable of being with her. I refused to burden her for the rest of her life.

I treated her badly. I can see that now. She didn't deserve someone like me, someone so full of rage, so dark and depressed, angry and wounded—someone incapable of considering anyone but himself.

There was no space in my head for her because all I could think about was getting over what had happened to me since I'd been in the coma. But now I understand why I was like that, why I didn't care about anything else.

It was for her. I did it for her.

I wanted to be the person I'd been before because that was the only way of getting her back, having her in my life, being able to love her the way she deserved. The way *we* deserved, finally having our shot, our opportunity, with nothing standing in our way.

For a year, I was a stranger to her.

She called, but I didn't pick up, and eventually she stopped calling.

I was thankful at first. It was a relief, because rejecting her over and over was killing me inside. But after a few days, I started pining away for another of those missed calls. If she'd given up, that could only mean one thing: Kam had moved on. Without me. Just as I had told her to.

Things were different with my brother. He was with me throughout my recovery. He never left my side, through all my fits of anger, all those moments when I wanted to throw in the towel.

"You've got to get her back, Thiago. Otherwise, what was the point of all this?" he told me one day when I was at my lowest and I really wanted to give up.

"I don't matter to her anymore," I said, taking a drag on my cigarette.

I'd started smoking again. It was stupid, but it was a stupid thing that helped me relax.

"The fact that she's living a normal life again doesn't mean that she doesn't love you. I've never seen anyone fight for someone the way she fought for you," Taylor said. "You mean everything to her. And as much as it hurts me to admit it, you need to be together. I know that. You've got to get her back, and to do that, you've got to get better."

So I did. And my brother was my rock. He came to see me whenever he could, and we spent hours together talking. I noticed that when Kam came up, it hurt less and less, but I also got scared when he told me she was looking good, hanging out with friends, going to basketball games, even partying.

What he never mentioned was whether she was going out with anyone, and I never asked.

I couldn't worry about that. I had to focus on my recovery above all else.

It took a whole year for my body to feel somewhat back to normal, and even then, I still hadn't made a complete recovery.

One day, my brother, my mother, and I were sitting on our front porch, enjoying the sun. I was complaining about my cane, which I still couldn't walk well without. Taylor said, "I don't know, man, I think it gives you some sex appeal. Like a professor or something."

Our mother couldn't help but beam as she looked back and forth between us.

"Do you?" I asked, lifting it up and poking him in the stomach with it.

His abs were rock-hard. He was still in such great shape. It was no surprise they'd just signed him for the NBA G League.

Being at home with them, joking and laughing, I felt like myself again. And I knew I couldn't keep being so negative.

I mean, we were alive, weren't we? And there were a lot of people in Carsville who couldn't say the same.

I had never told my mother about my encounter with Lucy. Or how I felt it was my little sister who had guided me through the school. How she had protected me, how we had made up for lost time while I was in a coma.

I hadn't been able to, because a part of me felt guilty for leaving Lucy and coming back. But now that I'd recovered, I knew my place was here and that Lucy would be OK.

I looked at my mother, and she was so happy, so calm at last, with the two of us beside her, that I knew it was time to tell her everything, strange or impossible as it might seem. I needed to get it off my chest, and she needed to know. It took a long time, but she listened attentively, and when I was done, I concluded, "Lucy's all right, Mom."

My brother had his back turned to us. I could imagine his eyes reddening from the effort not to cry. My mother, though, she seemed finally able to put an end to that story and move on. She reached up and stroked my cheek.

"I knew she'd take care of you," she said, "no matter what choice you made. I knew you'd be together."

"She told me to tell you she loves you and not to worry, because time there is different from time here. She told me when she saw you again, only a few days would have passed for her."

We didn't talk about it again.

We didn't have to. Telling my story, telling my mother and brother how I felt when we were together, helped us all turn the page.

It took me a while to gather the courage to go see Kami. Time stretched on until she had graduated with a degree in fine arts.

I didn't regret keeping my distance. We both needed time—to grow, to heal, to let things settle. It felt different. It felt right. Like maybe we finally had a shot at doing this the way we were meant to.

I showed up at Harvard the day after her graduation. I had no idea what her plans were or what she'd say when she laid eyes on me. I didn't know if she was in a relationship, whether she'd fallen in love with someone else or still thought about me.

I was scared. I can admit that.

But standing there at her door, I knew I'd done the right thing. I knew it deep in my heart. Whatever happened between us, I could at least say that I had come back from the dead for her. I'd come back thank to her. And that had to mean something, didn't it?

When she opened the door, I didn't recognize her at first. She had cut her hair and was wearing it in two braids. She was dressed in ripped jeans covered in paint, a black tank top with a red flannel shirt tied around her waist.

She opened the door, and everything seemed to stop.

She opened the door, and life held its breath.

Would she let me back in?

Would she let me love her the way I wanted?

Or would she close the door in my face.

I think you can guess what happened.

Can't you?

# CHAPTER TWENTY-EIGHT

## Kami

AT FIRST, I WAS PARALYZED. IT WAS AS IF I'D SEEN A GHOST. I examined every inch of his body, trying to find in him the guy I'd left lying in bed years ago—that weak, angry, irritable, bitter man who didn't know how to love me when I had set everything aside to bring him back, to make him live again.

It wasn't easy to reconcile that image with the person I saw now, but there he was, no denying it—tall and strong, with green eyes and tousled brown hair. It was Thiago, standing there before me, a cane in his right hand.

I felt…everything. I was flooded with emotions. But most of all, I was angry. I was angry because I couldn't be with him, because my life had changed, because he was no longer part of it, and most of all, because he was the one to make that decision, not me.

"Kam, can I—?"

"No," I cut him off. "You can't."

His green eyes looked me up and down and came to a stop on my face. He looked lost. Utterly lost.

"Just let me try and explain—"

"I don't want you to explain anything," I responded, gripping the door so tightly my fingers started to hurt. "There's nothing for you to say, nothing at all, because what we said in the past is what got us here, and dammit, if you look at me again and you open your mouth, my whole life will turn upside down and I can't, I just can't, OK? I'm sorry."

I tried to close the door, but he stopped me. "Please. Give me five minutes. Just five minutes."

I shook my head.

"I'm going to Europe, Thiago," I said, voice trembling. "I'm going for three months, and the last thing I want right now is for you to make me question something I've been planning a long time, something I deserve after so much pain, after all the studying and hard work, missing you and knowing you were never going to come back, waiting for you to call me and show up at this fucking door."

"Kam..."

"It's too late!" I shouted, losing my composure. "I'm sorry."

I tried to control myself, but I had to shut the door. I almost caved when I saw the sorrow in his eyes. I almost dropped everything to throw myself into his arms, but something inside me told me that I had to go on with my life. I couldn't abandon my plans.

And I didn't—at least, not for a while.

———

I traveled across Europe: in France, I walked along the Champs-Élysées and climbed the Eiffel Tower. I went to London and Scotland, and by the time I left, I'd even picked up the accent. I went to Berlin and soaked up the history. In Italy, I ate pasta until I thought I'd burst. I went to Prague and Luxembourg and enjoyed the beaches in Spain and learned to love that soup from Andalusia they call *salmorejo*. I fell in love with the sea in Greece and ran through the Austrian mountains like Empress Sissi and her sisters.

I rode on airplanes, trains, cars, and sat on the back of motorcycles. I grew, I thought, I matured, I cried, I yearned, I laughed, I met people I would hold forever in my heart, and when it was over, I knew that despite my pledge, despite all my efforts to let him go and close the door at last, I couldn't.

It didn't matter how many miles I put between us, how many seas separated us. In my head, Thiago was still there, sorrowful, asking me to talk, and I was still there shutting the door in his face.

I thought he deserved it; I thought it was what I was supposed to do. But who are we to deny what our heart yearns for?

Had he been wrong to push me away?

Of course, but I had been wrong to abandon myself to try to save him, because you can't forget who you are. He had done the right thing afterward; he had focused on himself, on getting better, getting stronger, while I was carrying around all that hurt and sorrow, forcing others to feel my pain. And in the end, all I managed to do was get lost along the way.

That trip to Europe opened my eyes, it helped me understand that nothing is the way you read in books, that there's no manual about how to love someone or how to get over a trauma. Every person is different, and the same decision could be good for one person and terrible for another. The only truth is that you have to live, because life is over in the blink of an eye and loving is meant to be something good, something that fills you with peace, something that makes you run off to the airport, jump in a taxi, pay a fortune to show up at a door not knowing what you're going to find there.

All I could do was hope—hope that he'd open the door for me. And when he did...

When he did, all I could do was take one step forward. One step toward him and cover his mouth with my hand and say what had been stuck in my throat since he showed up at my door.

"Don't say anything. If there's anything you want to tell me, anything at all—tell me with kisses."

# EPILOGUE ONE

## Kami

TWO YEARS LATER...

I OPENED MY EYES, AND THE SOFT RUMBLING SOUND brought me a feeling of infinite peace. I wasn't sure at first if I'd be able to handle this lifestyle. But after almost a year of living on the road, every day was full of joy and a thousand wonderful surprises.

We had fun outfitting the bus. Yes, the camper ended up being too small for us, so we bought a bus, the classic yellow bus all of us used to ride to school in.

We had to save a long time, and it took tons of work. I sold one of my best paintings to help Thiago pay for it. It was worth it. We turned it into our home, and a beautiful home it was. It was no mansion, of course, but we were together, and that was all we needed. He took care of the design and the grunt work; I focused on making it nice. And a year after starting our relationship over, we said goodbye to everyone we knew and set off on our adventure. I painted wherever we went, and Thiago worked on his start-up. He was in the early stages still, but he'd found three investors for a luxury RV rental project, and he was excited about the idea. If it took off, we'd stop having to pinch pennies so much, but we weren't in a rush: We were happy, we weren't lacking anything, and I loved waking up somewhere different every day. We went to art fairs where I tried to sell my work, and between that and Thiago's job, we made ends meet.

I woke up, propped my head up, and looked to the front of the bus. He was sitting at the wheel with a cup of coffee in the cup holder and his eyes on the road, leading…where?

I didn't know. I liked him surprising me with our next destination. I got out of bed, put on my bunny rabbit slippers, and smiled as I saw the breakfast he had prepared for me on the table. He always made breakfast, and he always arranged the eggs and avocado on my toast so they looked like a face. I grabbed my plate and my coffee and sat next to him. The road stretched on into infinity before us, and he looked over at me with excitement in his eyes.

"Good morning, beautiful," he said, turning for a kiss on the lips.

"Where are we headed?" I asked.

He laughed. He never told me. But I always asked.

"You'll see. You're going to love it."

I stared at him in silence. I couldn't help it. The way we loved each other was…I don't know how to explain it, really, but our love was bountiful. I felt as if my heart would burst with love every time he looked at me. I knew that he felt exactly the same about me.

How sweet, right? It's sweet when love is mutual, when it's healthy and respectful, when it's brave, passionate, and fun. Fun, especially. With time, I learned that Thiago had that in common with Taylor. He *was* fun, even if he'd hidden that part of himself for a long time.

Thiago was that guy who cracks jokes with a straight face, making him all that much more hilarious. And he loved me above all else, and he treated me like a queen.

It was hard at first to wipe the slate clean and start over. We argued a lot, then we'd patch things up in the worst possible way—or the best, depending on how you look at it: through sex.

A point came when we had to sit down and let out everything that was inside of us. It was a hard day, but it marked a before and after. We yelled at each other and cried, but then we consoled each other, and since then—since then, we've been rolling along fine. Literally, now that we're living on the road.

We barely saw Taylor that first year. We knew all he had accomplished, of course, because we talked on the phone, and I was happy to hear he was living his dream. He never had problems finding a date, but it made Thiago and me sad to realize that he still hadn't managed to fall in love. We felt guilty—me, especially.

We reached our destination: the Grand Canyon. But I was surprised when we parked the bus and Thiago told me we wouldn't be sleeping there. That was strange, because we always tried to save as much as possible, but at the same time, I wasn't going to say no to the fancy hotel where he had reserved two nights without telling me.

Our room had stunning views of the desert. As I was unpacking, looking for my toiletry bag before hopping in the shower, he went out to the balcony. To smoke, of course. He still needed his cane once in a while, but for the most part, he no longer used it. He'd gotten strong again, after his body had been so ravaged by the coma, and it turned me on and made me feel protected at the same time.

He leaned on the railing and enjoyed the view. But for me, just then, there was no sight better than him. I dropped what I was doing and went out there, standing beside him. He wrapped an arm around my shoulders and pulled me close, kissing me on the head.

We stood there admiring the landscape, then he asked me something strange: "Are you happy with me?"

Before answering, I looked into those precious green eyes. "What about you? Are you happy with me?"

He grinned and asked, "Are you ever going to stop answering my questions with another question?"

I shrugged. "I don't know. That's just one of my things."

"Kam, you've made me the happiest man in the world. Do you have any idea how many times I told myself I'd never get along with anyone? How many times I believed in my heart of hearts that no one could love me?"

I shook my head, but before I could respond, he kissed me and continued: "You have no idea. You have no idea how you make me feel—how much I love you. I love you so much it hurts sometimes. It hurts because it makes me feel weak. Not in a bad sense, but still, weak. My life, my heart, they're in your hands, Kam. You could break me into a million pieces just like that, and that used to terrify me, but at the same time, you were the one person who managed to reach me when I was practically dead. Do you realize how crazy that is?"

"It's just a reflection of how much I love you," I said.

He cupped my face and brought his lips to mine slowly. "Forever, right?" he asked.

I smiled. "Forever and beyond."

"What's beyond forever?" he asked.

"I don't know. You tell me. You're the one who's been there."

He kissed me, and I felt myself melting. It was a sweet kiss, gentle and full of love, and I never thought it would be the one right before he asked, "Will you marry me?"

He came out with it just like that, then stood back, waiting for a response.

He caught me off guard. I was in shock. Thiago was asking me to marry him? That didn't make sense; that wasn't who he was! For a moment, I thought it had been a spontaneous decision, but no. He reached into his pocket and pulled out a box. A ring! I couldn't believe it.

"This isn't just some crazy whim. I know what you're thinking," he said, nervously awaiting a reaction from me.

It was a delicate, elegant ring—simple, with a small diamond at the center. Discreet, perfect.

"When, though?" I asked. "How?"

"I bought the ring months ago in that little town up north that you liked so much, remember?"

I nodded, feeling overwhelmed with emotion.

"I waited to ask because I wanted to do it in a special

way, in a special place, but then I realized the more I planned, the less special it might be for you, so I've just been carrying it around in my pocket since then. I knew I would feel it when the moment came, and here it is."

A tear slid down my cheek as I simultaneously smiled like an idiot.

"I love you so much," I said, feeling my whole body trembling from emotion, nerves, surprise, infinite love. Then I realized he was still waiting for an answer. "Yes, of course, of course I'll marry you!"

He held me tight, then picked me up and spun me around.

We started kissing passionately and had to force ourselves to stop so he could slide the ring onto my finger.

And then everything made sense. Everything. Meeting when we were little, the long separation, the reunion, our fights, losing each other, getting each other back. All those years had brought us to this moment, and it was then that I could finally forgive myself.

Forgiveness freed me. It allowed me to breathe easy again and to keep moving forward, to start from zero with the man I loved and was anxious to build a life with.

Maybe it wasn't normal what we were doing, him and me and our bus, with no predetermined route, but it didn't matter, because we were alive and we were together, at last.

We made love that night—slowly, fully, like we didn't want the moment to end. But finally we fell asleep, and I knew there in that hotel bed that everything was how it should be.

We had loved each other softly...in secret...and with millions of kisses.

# EPILOGUE TWO

## Taylor

I GUESS WE DON'T ALL GET THE *HAPPILY EVER AFTER*. OUT on the court, I could see them laughing and kissing each other. They even showed up on the damn Kiss Cam. But don't worry. It didn't hurt the way it used to. I had gotten over it. I really had.

It had been tough for me in the past, but now it was nice to see them together—she looked radiant, and my brother, he was basically drooling over her.

It was just the lovey-dovey shit that was nauseating.

Anyway, I had my own life, and by my own life, I mean basketball. I'd made it into the NBA. I was playing with the Boston Celtics and earning that NBA money.

My life had made a 180-degree turn. I had a million-dollar condo in downtown Boston and was traveling all over the world, winning games—sometimes losing them—and living a life most people could only dream of. But it was also lonely.

Most of my teammates were either married or hooking up with anything that moved (I did that, too, but not all the time). But even with all the traveling and riches, what I really missed was affection.

I'm not going to cry about it or anything, but I hadn't experienced anything like what I'd felt for Kami with any other woman, and I was starting to ask myself if it was my fate to be alone.

How pathetic.

That was on my mind one morning, a morning when I was supposed to close one of the most important endorsement contracts of my career, and I had to do it with *her*. I couldn't stand her, with her air of superiority, the way she was always telling me not to let fame get to my head, the way she bossed me around. Just the other day, she'd said that if Nike told me to get the swoosh tattooed on my forehead, I'd better do it—that was the first time she mentioned they might sponsor me.

She was the daughter of a big shareholder in the Celtics, so you can imagine the type we're talking about. When I met her, I remember thinking she was hot, with her penetrating black eyes, but not two minutes later, she opened her mouth, and I lost interest. I would have preferred another agent, but how was I going to refuse an offer from Jack Gates's daughter? If he said she was the one I needed, I had to bow my head and say yes, especially being the new guy who was still proving himself.

We met at her office, and I couldn't help noticing what she was wearing: a black tube dress and stiletto heels to try to make herself look a little taller than a Minion. Every time I saw her, she seemed to have a different pair on. Sexy as they were, my takeaway was how much of a complex she might have about being five foot two. Sometimes, to get on her nerves, I liked to stand and lean over her desk to make her feel small—that wasn't like me, but her *goddess of negotiations* attitude made me want to do it. She knew she was the one who held the reins. And she loved throwing that in my face.

"Good morning, Di Bianco," she said, taking out papers and spreading them across the desk. "Here's the contract we've finalized with Nike."

I sat down to read it over. When I realized it was more than thirty pages, I looked up at her and said, "You're kidding, right?"

"Too many pages for your little brain?"

I threw the contract down and scowled at her. She grinned.

"I'm sorry," she said. "That was taking it too far."

"I have an engineering degree from Harvard, top of my class. I'm not just some dumb jock."

"And just like everyone who went to Harvard, you can't help but mention it," she said, raising a perfectly sculpted eyebrow.

OK, that stung, but I just wanted to get down to business. "Can we stop the pissing contest and talk about what I'm here for?" I asked.

"I'll ignore the vulgarity and get to the point: Nike wants you."

"And what about you? Do you want me, too?" I asked, not knowing where the hell that had come from.

"All I want from you is your signature on this contract I've been negotiating for months."

"How much are they paying?" I asked.

"A million a year."

"You did your homework," I responded, impressed. That was a lot of money.

"That's what I wanted to talk to you about," she said, sitting on the desk and looking at me with those glassy eyes that were so sexy it was hard not to imagine her down on her knees—

"I want to up my percentage on this."

When she said that, all erotic thoughts disappeared from my mind. "What? Are you crazy?" I asked, almost choking.

She didn't even blink. "If it wasn't for me, you wouldn't—"

"If it wasn't for you, I'd just have a different agent."

"Yeah," she said, "another agent who would have no hope whatsoever of getting you this kind of deal your first season on a team."

"You don't know that."

"I damn well do know that. Who do you think talked to my father to get him to pull strings at Nike—telling them you were the next big thing? You may think a million bucks is a lot of money, but if you show who you are out there on the court, you could be looking at three times that in a few years."

We didn't say anything for a moment, but I hadn't failed to notice she was complimenting me. "You talked to your father about me?" I asked.

She blushed slightly, and I wondered what planet I was on. Her, blushing? I'd always thought she had ice in her veins. "It's part of my job," she responded. "I observe, I make assessments."

"You break guys' balls."

She hit the desk with her tiny fist to keep from laughing. "Will you just say yes and sign?"

"I don't know, I think I might need something to sweeten the deal."

"Something more than a million dollars?"

I stretched my arms up in the air, pretending to yawn.

"Am I boring you?" she asked with a scowl.

"No, but I could use a massage. My back's been killing me," I responded.

"Careful, Di Bianco," she warned me.

I bent forward and looked closely at her, at those thick eyelashes, those carmine lips.

"Or what?" I asked, surprised again at how gorgeous she was.

"Or I can make your life on this team a living hell," she said without skipping a beat.

"Damn," I replied with a laugh, "you're actually scaring me."

She got off the desk and ripped the contract from my hands. "Either you accept my offer, or it's bye-bye to this contract," she said, getting ready to tear it up.

"Not even you would be capable—" I began, and then I saw she wasn't bluffing. She really was ready to rip it in half. "What the fuck?"

"You play with fire, you might get burned, Taylor."

"You're honestly willing to give up all that work?"

"You think I can't find other players to represent?"

"I'm a future star, you said it yourself, and I know it's not just dumb luck that you chose me to work with. You're like me. You want the best."

We stared at each other for a few long seconds.

"Sign the damn contract, bump me up to 30 percent, and the offer's back on the table," she said, very sure of herself.

I hesitated, then responded, "I'll sign, but with one condition," and I lifted a finger to emphasize that. "You have to be my date to my brother's wedding."

I observed her reaction: first a blank stare, then a long exhalation, then a look of something like relief. "I didn't know you had a brother."

"I've got my secrets. I'm curious now what you thought I was going to ask."

"Nothing," she said, putting the contract back on her desk. "I'll go. I mean, it's pathetic that you can't get a date without extorting someone, but you're pathetic, so no surprises there. Now sign."

She looked like she wanted to wrap things up, but I circled the desk and stood in front of her. She had to crane her neck up to look at me.

"What did you think I was going to say?" I asked again. I was starting to get a handle on the dynamic between us, and if she thought I was the kind of guy to abuse my position, I needed to make it clear that wasn't my intention at all. "Answer me, Victoria." That was the first time since we'd met that I'd called her by her first name.

That got a strange reaction—almost a flinch—and she responded, "Sign it, Taylor." And when I watched those lips move, I felt a stab of pain between my legs. I was dying to kiss her—to bite that fleshy lip and feel her tongue wrapping around mine. I had to control myself, dammit.

I grabbed the pen she handed me, bent down, and signed the agreement, increasing the percentage of her earnings. Now she grinned, and my face started to feel warm.

"A pleasure doing business with you," she said, turning her back and slipping the contract into a file folder.

Before walking out, I turned back to her. "Vic, I'd never ask you to do anything you weren't comfortable with. I'm sorry if it came across that way. Anyway, I know the day will come when you'll be the one begging me for it."

I couldn't stop myself after what she'd just made me feel—and I was intentionally getting under her skin. The first day we met, she'd told me, *Don't call me Vic.* She always had a snappy answer for everything. But not this time. As I walked out, I couldn't believe what I had said. Had I really hinted to the daughter of one of the team's owners that I thought she was hot for me? And what did it mean that she didn't respond?

*Jesus, Taylor, as soon as you pull out of one thing, you get stuck in another.*

Hey! Don't be perverted, I didn't mean it that way.

Or…maybe I did.

# Acknowledgments

Ten books already! Who'd have ever thought? It's been almost four years since I published *My Fault*, since my life's dream came true, and it's still hard for me to believe. I'll never forget those months when I uploaded my book to Wattpad and my first-ever readers made comments and asked me for more. I never thought I'd make it this far, and I have to thank everyone who's contributed to me becoming the writer I am today.

Thanks to my editors, Rosa and Ada and the entire team at Penguin Random House, for the opportunity to reach places I never thought possible.

Thank you to Christa, Brittany, Holly, and the rest of the amazing team at Sourcebooks for your support and for believing in my books.

Thanks to my family, who helped me and listened when I didn't think I would finish on time. You're my biggest supporters, and I love all of you like crazy. And thanks to my team of express readers: my cousin Bar and my sisters Ro and Belén, who finished this book in a few hours and gave their much-needed opinions so I could make this trilogy the best it could possibly be.

Bar, you're always there, despite the distance, and I swear, without you these books would never be what they are. Thanks for your sincerity and your comments.

Thanks to you, Joaquín, for being my best companion and putting up with me during hard times.

And finally, thank you, again, for still being there, for giving me your time, letting me astound you, make you fall in love, make you cry, make you suffer—because without a little suffering, what would a book be? I truly hope you've enjoyed this and that you'll give me another chance to surprise you... But give me a few months at least. ;)

I love you all!

Till next time!

# About the Author

Mercedes Ron is a *New York Times* and #1 international bestselling author with over five million copies sold and translations into more than twelve languages. Her hit Culpables (My Fault) trilogy became a global phenomenon and has been adapted into multiple record-breaking-viewership international films, with additional adaptations of her Dímelo series (Tell Me) and her Enfrentados (Face to Face) books currently underway. Born in Argentina, Mercedes now lives in Seville with her husband and their beloved dog. Follow her on Instagram @mercedesronn and TikTok at @mercedesron.